Vicky's Victory

—

Malt Shop Milestones
Book One

—

Nadine C. Keels

Vicky's Victory

Nadine. A French name, meaning, "hope."

Nadine C. Keels is an author and blogger with a lifelong passion for the power of story. She writes the kinds of stories she wants to read but can't always find, and her aim is to spark hope and inspiration in as many people as she can reach.

—

<u>Malt Shop Milestones Series</u>
Vicky's Victory | Berta's Bounceback | Ari's Aria

—

<u>Crowns Legacy Series</u>
Reviving the Commander | Embracing the Outcast

—

<u>Eubeltic Realm Series</u>
Eubeltic Descent | Eubeltic Quest | Eubeltic Virtue | Eubeltic Outliers

—

<u>Hope Beyond Series</u>
Eminence | Simplicity

—

<u>Movement of Crowns Series</u>
The Movement of Crowns | The Movement of Rings | The Movement of Kings

—

<u>For Every Love Series</u>
Love Unfeigned | Hope Unashamed | Kiss and 'Telle?

—

<u>Heartstrings Series</u>
We Were Real | A Christmas So Real

—

<u>Jhoi Series</u>
World of the Innocent | World of Joy

—

Love by the Breather: Four Romantic Reads

---✺---

*To my mother, Roberta V. Keels,
a classic woman who'll always be cooler than me,
and to my father, Michael C. Keels,
a guitarist, jazz aficionado, and the reason why I've had classic
jazz in my bones since before I knew what bones are*

Chapter One

FOR HER TO HAVE SUDDENLY imagined dancing—and to imagine being dipped, no less—in the middle of Bro Brown's Burgers and Malts? *Oh, mercy.* That had been silly.

Vicky Phillips was still at Bro Brown's now on this Saturday afternoon, seated in a booth, sipping a strawberry ice cream soda from a tall glass. The height of lunch hour was over, so the crowd in here was light. Music was swinging from the jukebox on one side of the room, but Vicky barely heard it, her mind passing through belated thoughts. Belated memories of a pair of noisy children, running around outside together.

She reached up to touch one side of her honey brown face, feeling the pleasant warmth those memories caused. In a way they never had before.

Her daydreaming carried on in a forward direction until two of her girlfriends arrived at Bro Brown's.

"Hey, Vicky!" Berta and Evie waved at her before the two of them went up to the front counter to make their orders. The girls would surely be brimming with chitchat once they joined

Vicky at her table, and she'd best be ready to chitchat back. Any odd silence from her, and her friends were bound to start asking questions. Then Vicky would be likely to blurt the news about an, um, incident that had taken place here, not too many minutes ago.

If the incident could even be called news. It might not have been anything after all. Maybe it wouldn't have felt like it could be something, if not for a (coincidental?) conversation Vicky had been a part of, a few months back.

See, somehow a certain subject had come up around the breakfast table at the Phillips family's house one Sunday morning. Vicky's father had been in one of his jaunty moods, saying at one point in the discussion, "He doesn't have to know how to dance. A man just has to make sure he picks a woman who knows how. Then when they're on the dance floor, while she's doing her thing, all he has to do is get a little low and snap his fingers to her feet." He lowered one hand and threw down some upbeat snaps near his side. "Makes it look like somethin'."

Vicky's older brother, Roy, had snickered. "Oh, so while Mom was busy bopping around and kicking up her heels and everything, you used to just stand there snapping at her?"

"Hey." A smirk quirked up the dark, trim mustache on their father's mahogany face. "I didn't say *I* didn't know how to dance. The band would be wore out by the time I was done on the floor. Still happens when I take your mother out. Ask anybody."

Vicky's mother cut into the conversation after crunching into a strip of bacon. "All right now, saints. Is this really the subject we need to have on our minds right before church?"

"Hm? Why not?" her husband wanted to know. "Don't we talk about the Bible at church? They danced in the Bible, Sister Phillips. Amen?"

"No 'amen' to that. That's not the kind of dancing you're going on about."

"No? You don't know what all their dances looked like in the Bible. Who's to say that sometimes God's children weren't jukin'?"

"Otis!" Vicky's mother squeaked at her husband, her eyes popping wide with the appropriate degree of Sabbath Day disapproval.

"Marion?" he addressed his wife in return with an innocent lift of his eyebrows, until her light brown cheeks twitched with what was, no doubt, loosely locked-up laughter.

Vicky swallowed a bite of her scrambled eggs, holding up a hand to get her father's attention. "Wait, Dad, come on. A guy won't get by for that long on the floor if he can't dance. What if his girl wants him to pick her up and swing her around and stuff?"

"Ain't hard to swing a girl around," her father claimed. "He can even do a test run beforehand. Any old day when he sees her, he can bump right smack into her, catch her before she falls. See what her weight feels like. Then he'll know he can swing her."

Roy snorted.

Vicky turned amused eyes on her mother. "Is that what Dad did to you? Ran up and barreled into you one day, then the next day he asked you to dance and swung you around?"

Not meeting her daughter's eyes, Vicky's mother kept her gaze leveled on her now grinning husband sitting across the breakfast table from her. After some slow chewing of her bacon, she answered, "No, Victoria. Your father did not." She reached out to pick up her cup of coffee. "It was me who used to swing *him* around."

By the end of that Sunday morning exchange with the family, Vicky had been laughing.

Now, these months later, it would take a tad of extra effort for her to laughingly settle into an afternoon chat with her friends. To move on, sort of, from today's earlier, um, incident.

This day was the last Saturday of summer break before Vicky's junior year of high school would start. She, Berta, and Evie had planned ahead to meet here at Bro Brown's, a spot located on Main Street in West Hill, a community nicknamed the "Black Diamond district."

As Berta and Evie were approaching Vicky's table with their own tall glasses to sip from and a side of potato fries to share, Louis Jordan and His Tympany Five jumped onto the jukebox, urging everybody in the place to "Let the Good Times Roll."

Berta harrumphed as she slid into the booth beside Vicky, saying, "Uh huh. If they really wanted the good times to roll on for us, they'd push school back a few weeks. Or months. Till after Christmas."

Evie slid into the booth on the opposite side of the table. "I'm glad school's starting up," she admitted, her voice dropping a notch with her eyes. "It'll help give my family something else to talk about at the dinner table."

In response to that, Vicky's heart also dropped a little. Evie's great-grandmother, her family's matriarch almost halfway across the country, had passed away recently. The past few weeks at home hadn't been the easiest for Evie.

Vicky reached across the table to give her friend's hand a quick squeeze, saying, "That's different." Berta hummed quiet agreement beside her, and once a faint smile of thanks came to Evie's lips, Vicky went on. "I'm glad about school too, since I've decided to join the paper this year."

Berta shook her head, making the curls at the ends of her dark brown hair jiggle. "The school paper. Leave it to you," she said, giving another playful harrumph. "Being the only kid with all A's every term isn't enough for you. You have to go and pick a club that comes with bonus homework for *fun*."

Vicky laughed at that. "It's not about piling on more homework." After taking another sip of creamy strawberry, she told her friends, "I want to be a journalist."

That announcement made Evie pause from taking a sip from her own glass. "You mean as a job?"

"Mm hm. A career. After college." Vicky waved a hand toward Bro Brown's front windows, through which more of Main Street's establishments were visible. "I bet I wouldn't even have to leave Black Diamond. I could work for the *Courier*."

Berta dipped a pair of potato fries into her malted milkshake as she slowly asked, "Do any ladies work there now?"

Vicky looked from one of her friends to the other, recognizing the hesitance on their faces. She put a hand to her chest. "If Ida B. Wells could be a journalist back in her day, I can now."

Berta raised a teasing eyebrow at her. "Now?"

Tipping her head toward Berta, Vicky conceded to the tease with a mild roll of her eyes. "After college."

Evie chortled across the table, grabbing a fry to dip.

Berta munched on her crispy potato pair, then she drummed her fingertips down on the tabletop to shift course. "Well, you have plenty of other business to deal with before then," she told Vicky, pointing between her and Evie. "Y'all know how Chester Cunningham had that big fight with Hester this summer?"

Evie clicked her tongue. "Oh, the match made in money," she reflected aloud. In a dreamy gesture, she brought the back of her hand up to her forehead, near the decorative headscarf tied in a bow around her black hair. "Who'd have thought Chester and Hester wouldn't last forever?"

Berta's look took on a sly quality. "Yeah, well, he must be over that already. 'Cause I heard from the bag boy at the grocery who found out at the filling station that Chester's been hinting around town about our own Vicky Phillips."

Evie gasped.

Vicky's jaw dropped. "Really?"

Berta gave a satisfied nod. "Really."

Surprise and feminine instinct almost led Vicky to reach up to her head of carefully curled brown hair, to check on at least one of the two large rolls smoothed up on either side of her head.

At some point after the last World War ended, it occurred to Vicky that she'd begun to see fewer among America's female population still wearing their hair in the way she'd chosen today. She understood that fashionable trends moved along with time, but she hadn't gotten away from styling her hair like this when the mood would strike her. With those ample swirls pinned in place up there, topping off her appearance, she never felt more like a young lady wearing a crown.

Right now, though, she remembered there wasn't any need for her to check her hair on account of the Chester in question. Not only because he wasn't there but because, once the surprise and an initially flattered sensation bubbled up and fizzled out of her, Vicky was—

"Not interested." One decided shake of her head accompanied her statement.

Evie looked incredulous. "You're not interested?" She brought a fist down to rest on her hip. "The richest, finest boy on the hill has his eye on you, and you're not interested?"

Berta's lips bunched up with an objection. "Who says he's the finest?" she challenged, as she was the one in their trio who had a boyfriend. A fellow by the name of Howard.

Evie shrugged a shoulder. "Chester sure ain't ugly. And anyway, with all he'll inherit as a Cunningham? That could make any boy look mighty fine."

Before this chat could spiral any deeper into dollar signs and fine looks that weren't Vicky's concern, she felt the need to reemphasize, "Not interested."

Berta didn't appear convinced. "We've been sixteen for a while now, Vick. Didn't you get permission to start dating on your birthday?"

"Yes, I did. And I do want to start." Vicky's eyes narrowed a bit. "But Chester? He hardly even talks to me, outside of a 'hello' once in a while, or 'Oh, look! It's raining outside.' Doesn't it seem suspicious that he would turn his attention to me, of all people, out of the blue?"

"What's so suspicious about that?" Berta replied, pointing Vicky out with an open hand, up and down. "The Brain of West Hill High."

Vicky gave a weak grunt at the title she hadn't asked for, which didn't seem to make any difference to all the people who used it to refer to her. "I don't know why folks make that kind of fuss." She held up a couple of her fingers. "We've still got two whole years of high school ahead. As I go along, my grades could slip."

Evie's face deadpanned at her. "You planning on letting your grades slip?"

Well. Vicky's supposition had sounded flimsy to even her own ears. She lowered her fingers. "No." *Never, hopefully.* "But it's still two years."

Berta wasn't moved. "So? Either way, you're The Brain 'round these parts. When you think about it, besides Hester, you're just about the most popular girl at school."

Vicky swept that assertion away with one hand. "Being known for your grades doesn't mean you're popular. And I wouldn't trust the word about Chester. If he's hinting around like he's moved on from Hester already, it could be all jive. Trying to make her jealous or something." She wagged a finger in the air, another squint coming to her eyes. "Besides, have y'all ever listened to him talk? Really listened? He's got this attitude like he can have anything he wants."

Berta's forehead wrinkled. "Well, he can buy just about anything he wants. At least around here."

"No, I mean *anything*-anything. He could be thinking he'll woo the smart girl at school with presents and fancy dates, so then she'll do his homework for him."

Evie's look was skeptical. "You don't know if he'd do that."

"But I've seen his attitude, though. I don't trust it." Vicky's gaze settled down on her soda before her, her fingers wandering in to twist the glass this way and that by its base. "I really do want to start dating, but I don't want to step out with just anybody."

Berta's half-nod wasn't a full concession. "Fair enough. So what kind of guy do you want, then?"

Vicky stared at her glass without seeing it, her daydreams beginning to slip back to the forefront. "Oh, say... A guy who can be sweet. And—" Her eyes came up to move cautiously between her friends. "You'll think this is corny."

Evie leaned forward. "Tell us."

After an additional moment of indecision, Vicky came clean. "I dream about going on library dates."

Neither of her friends said anything right away. Then Evie was the one to speak, low in volume, her measure of humor under control but still there. "So, doing homework isn't only fun for you. It's your idea of romance too." She clasped her hands together before her chest, breathing out her next words with a high sigh. "And there, the handsome prince caught the beautiful princess's eye over their history notes and math problems. Doves perched on the windowsill outside. The violins started up. It was love! Then ol' Miss Tatum came over from behind the front desk and told the violins to '*Shh!* Stop that! This is the library.'"

A titter escaped Berta.

Vicky couldn't help smiling at her own expense, but she went on with insistence. "I just mean a guy who matches me *here*." She tapped a finger to her temple. "A guy who'll match me and who'll like the idea of me working as a writer someday. I want him to be interesting and to think I'm interesting too."

"Oh, my lovebug," Evie said, sending a gentle smile Vicky's way. "Boys our age aren't interested in us yet. Not deep like that. Right now, they only want girls around for a good time."

Berta's eyes enlarged. "Thanks, Evelyn!" She threw up her hands in dramatic fashion.

Evie directed a gesture of acknowledgment toward a Howard who wasn't present as she told his girlfriend, "Oh, you know what I mean. Boys in general. They want to have fun right now." She then turned urging eyes on Vicky. "We girls can have our fun too, you know. Going on dates with a guy doesn't mean you have to marry him. For instance, you could go to the homecoming dance with Chester, if he asks you, and that could be that. It'd be a nice first date, right? A school function, lots of people." She indicated the three of them at the table. "Including us."

The homecoming dance. There it was. The kind of topic to get Vicky's insides stirring in a way they never quite had, before today. "I'm not sure about that kind of thing yet..." she told her friends, her voice barely above a whisper.

Finally, she was unable to help it any longer. Her thoughts slipped back to today's earlier, um, incident.

Chapter Two

WHEN VICKY HAD ARRIVED at Bro Brown's before her friends that day, she'd immediately stopped off at the jukebox.

Pulling her coin purse out of her small shoulder bag, she dug out a coin, dropped it into the jukebox, and punched in a selection to add to the song sequence. She then began making her way toward the front counter, fiddling with her coin purse some more. Some of her change slipped out of the purse and out of her grip, dropping to the black and white checkered floor, rolling under an unoccupied table. After bending down to retrieve her change, Vicky partially straightened up without looking ahead of her right away.

At that moment, Willie, the teenaged son of the chief cook who owned Bro Brown's, was at the climax of an animated story he was telling a friend of his. Though Willie's friend was seated, Willie was standing up and moving in reverse. His feet were a flashing deck of cards in swift shuffle as he angled backward, lifting an arm as if getting ready to hurl an invisible brick. Or to launch an invisible football.

His friend, seeing behind him, was too late in throwing up a warning wave. Hence, Willie, in the middle of his energized shuffling, backed right up into Vicky.

Now, she wasn't a featherweight of a girl. But Willie was fairly tall in stature, a varsity athlete with a frame that rated somewhere between husky and hulky.

Nature dictated that when such a large Willie would bump into an unprepared Vicky with that much momentum, the Vicky would be the one to topple over.

"Oh!" Vicky tripped sideways in her saddle shoes. She was going down.

But then, she wasn't.

She'd only reached a leaning mid-topple when Willie turned in time for his hands to scoop down, catching her around her back, halting her fall.

"Aw, man—sorry!" Willie was quick to apologize but not too quick to let go. He winced as he discovered the unintended recipient of his backward bump. "You okay, Vicky?"

In an unusual daze, she blinked up into the anxious expression on the rich brown face hovering over her.

For almost as long as Vicky could remember, Willie Brown had been nothing less or more to her than one of the boys in the neighborhood. During Vicky's younger years, back when Willie's mother was still alive, Vicky would sometimes go over to the Browns' house with her own mother. As Mrs. Phillips and Mrs. Brown would visit, they'd inevitably send little ears away to stay out of grown folks' business. Vicky would then take off to play outside with Willie, the two of them noisily running around doing a bunch of nothing in the way that children do much better than grown folks ever could.

As the years passed, however, Vicky and Willie didn't spend much time together. Their everyday social circles didn't always overlap. But she was still pretty aware of when he gained two key distinctions around town.

Firstly, Willie was recognized as the rising star of West Hill High School football and one of the standout athletes of intermural sports in the region. Vicky enjoyed attending her school's home games with her friends. While she was no expert on sports, she could tell for herself that Willie was indeed a talented football player.

Secondly, Willie turned out to be the first boy in his high school class who could grow a beard.

One weekend, someone or other walking past the front windows of the barbershop had spotted him in there. Rather than getting the usual close cut for his black hair at that moment, Willie was lying back in the tilted barber chair, getting a bona fide shave. On his face. With the barber's real razor and shaving cream and everything.

Word about it got around school the next week. Willie eventually confessed, confirming the truth of it all.

His status as the first among his teenaged peers to start shaving came in handy at school, given that there was another Willie in the same class. For whatever reason, fellow students didn't use the Willies' different last names, Parks and Brown, to distinguish between the two. And West Hill's young generation wouldn't be so formal as to stick to the Willies' full first names: *William* (Parks) and *Willard* (Brown).

Instead, when differentiation between the two was required in conversation, Willie Parks was "Willie," and Willie Brown was "Willie with the Beard."

A moniker that blended into practically one word, pronounced in an automatic flow off the tongue.

"Hear about yesterday? Mrs. Judkins ran out of gas in the middle of Main."

"Yeah? How'd she get her car to the filling station? Or did she?"

"Yeah, she did. Willie-with-the-Beard and some of them guys came and pushed the car down the street for her."

It was like that. Didn't even matter that Willie actually maintained a clean-shaven face. The fact that he *could* grow out a beard if he wanted to—that was the thing.

Granted, now that Willie and his class were entering their senior year, he was no longer the only one among them who had to shave regularly. But he remained the only one at school whom others addressed by the Beard.

Yet, for the few prolonged seconds that Vicky remained leaning in Willie's hold in the midst of the light crowd at Bro Brown's, she wasn't thinking about beards. Or about football. Or even about two noisy little kids running around doing a bunch of nothing outside, back in the day.

Rather, Vicky was thinking about dancing.

Which, of course, was silly. Silly because her father had intentionally been ridiculous those months ago, making up that stuff about guys bumping right smack into girls on purpose for potential dancing reasons. Willie apparently hadn't even noticed her come in here, and she'd hardly paid him notice either. Otherwise, she probably could have saved herself from getting bumped into in the first place.

Besides, it was as plain as anything that such a Willie would never have needed to do a test to see if he'd be able to lift and swing a Vicky all right. A fact that was plain even before he'd stopped her toppling just now.

And another reason why her thinking about dancing was silly? Vicky, personally, wasn't someone who danced. Not the guy-and-girl kind of dancing.

Her parents would go out and dance. Not as often as when they were young, but they still did. Her brother would go off on his own outings to dance too. Her friends were no exceptions, attending homecomings and community youth dances and such.

But Vicky had yet to ever venture to do so herself. It'd made no difference that chaperoned dances at school and whatnot hadn't fallen under her parents' rule about her not dating until she turned sixteen. She could have started attending dances well before now, if she'd wanted, though she hadn't felt it necessary to share that detail with anyone.

Vicky had always imagined she'd be too self-conscious for dancing with a partner. It wouldn't be the same as all the times she danced by herself or played at partnering with her friends or her brother. Partnering with a guy at an actual dance? That would be serious business. Business that would likely be nerve-racking for her.

She'd heard plenty about dance floors bursting with vibrant jazz. Couldn't a girl who was brand new to the floor wind up stumbling or falling flat on her face in the heat of the jazzy action?

Then there were the slower songs. While a guy was holding her, where was Vicky supposed to look? Would her partner's gazing into her eyes become awkward after a minute? Sure, she could look past him instead, over his shoulder or something.

But would looking around the room at other people distract her, making the moment less romantic?

Or maybe it wasn't supposed to be romantic in any real way, if it was only a dance. Only a social event. But what if the music gave her lovey-dovey feelings for her dance partner, and it turned out that he didn't feel anything?

Books, on the other hand—those were what Vicky knew. She drew such pleasure and inspiration from literature. From poetry. From the compelling use of language. Wouldn't it be much easier and more likely for her to get a real taste of romance through sharing the written word? For her heart to connect with a guy's as the two of them pored over books together? They might be studying for school or for other work. Or they could be sitting outdoors in the park together on a weekend afternoon, reading purely for (yes!) the fun of it.

Plus, during cozy reading sessions with a guy, Vicky would be in no danger of falling on her face in a roomful of dancers who'd be better on their feet. Dancers who'd be gawking if she made a fool of herself.

All of those possibilities were separate matters, though. Matters that should have nothing to do with the past few seconds at Bro Brown's, where Vicky and Willie were not dancing. He hadn't purposely dipped her into this hold she was leaning into.

With one of her hands clutching her shoulder bag against her, she didn't realize her free hand had taken a tight grip on Willie's plaid shirt until he set her upright on her feet.

"You okay?" he asked again, and she unclasped her fingers from his shirt. He released his hold on her then, and she felt a bit sorry that her past few seconds of leaning had come to an end.

A strange enough feeling for her to have, when it seemed she should have felt embarrassed instead. Willie's father was out of sight, likely back there with the second cook in the kitchen, but the clerk at the counter and the handful of other people in here had to have seen Vicky's near-spill and all. She went about checking herself over, brushing her hands along her skirt and short-sleeved blouse.

"Vicky."

Willie's low utterance of her name all but took her off guard. Her hands paused from fussing about her as she looked up at him. "Yes?" she replied, startled by the somewhat breathless state of her voice.

Although he still appeared concerned, faint amusement had come to edge the corners of Willie's mouth. He tipped his head a tad closer to her. "Are you okay?" he inquired a third time, his voice still low.

"Oh. Yes." Vicky glanced downward, only then noticing that Willie was holding up her coin purse. She must have dropped it and missed Willie picking it up for her. She accepted it back from him, hoping no more of her change had fallen out. She wasn't going to go crawling around for it in front of Willie. "I'm fine. Thank you."

He seemed relieved, his voice rising back to a normal level. "Gee, I'm sorry about that. I know a big ol' freight truck like me ought to watch where he's going."

A spurt of air that wasn't sure if it should be a laugh broke through Vicky's lips. She couldn't tell whether or not Willie was complimenting his size by the truck comparison.

He pointed a thumb behind him toward the front counter. "Say, how about if I get you something? You hungry? Up for a burger?"

"What?" Vicky found herself taken aback by his offer. "Oh, no, I—"

"Already had lunch, huh? You feel like a vanilla malt, then? Or chocolate?"

Vicky held up a hand to slow him down. "No, thank you, Willie. That's all right. I'm about to meet some friends here. They'll be here any minute."

"Oh? Oh." Willie stopped pointing behind him, his hand drifting in uncertainty before it curled into a loose ball, landing thoughtfully into his opposite palm. "Well, I can't knock you over like that and then do...nothing."

The earnest tone of his comment gave Vicky pause. A rather lovely kind of pause she couldn't have anticipated.

Before she knew it, she was smiling up at Willie and telling him, "Then, uh, let's just say you can owe me a favor. For later, sometime." She held her free hand out to him. "All right?"

Only a second passed before he smiled back, taking the hand that she extended. "All right," he said as the two of them shook on it. He then let go and reached for her shoulders, giving them a light squeeze and a pat. "Nice, um, bumping into you."

That brought a laugh from Vicky. "Real nice," was the reply that flew right out of her mouth ahead of her thoughts, and Willie was the one who paused this time.

A curious tilt came to his lips before his smile grew, a short chuckle rumbling from him.

Vicky caught on to her comment too late to prevent it. To her thinking, she didn't take the comment back, but she did add what she would have said instead, if she'd caught herself sooner. "You too."

As Willie stepped out of her way so that she could continue on toward the counter, his friend, another member of West Hill's varsity football team, was now getting up from his seat.

"Hey, Bam," Vicky greeted him.

"Hi, Vicky," he answered with a nod. "Thrilling as Willie's story was, I'm sorry I didn't stop him fast enough. First game's this Friday, though. You shoulda told him he owes you free tickets for crashing into you."

"Ah. Maybe next time." Vicky smiled and moved past Bam. Once she made it to the front counter, she didn't have to check the menu to know what she wanted to order. "A pink cow, please."

While she was waiting for her ice cream soda, she checked behind her over her shoulder, seeing Willie and Bam making their departure from Bro Brown's. Before Willie was fully out the door, he looked back over his shoulder as well, flashing a grin at Vicky.

Oh! My. Did her stomach actually jump in response? It would almost make her think she'd never been grinned at before...

VICKY WAS NOW FINISHING her soda ahead of her friends, as she'd had more time to work on hers.

She still didn't know how much of anything that incident truly was, or if anything would come of it. And, again, she and Willie hadn't been dancing or anything. So was it worth saying anything about it?

"You're not sure about what kind of thing yet?" Berta asked her. "Going out with Chester just for fun? Or going to the homecoming dance?"

Vicky again looked from one of her friends to the other, her stomach giving another sudden jump.

The dance.

She definitely wasn't sure about the dance.

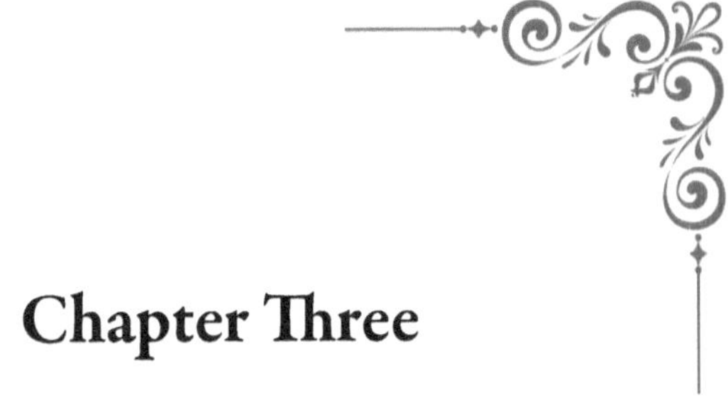

Chapter Three

THE FIRST, SHORT WEEK of school had gotten off to a wonderful start.

It was Friday afternoon now, and although classes were over, the day's school-related activities weren't over for Vicky. Later on, she and her friends would be riding along in a caravan to their football team's opening game of the season. The first time Vicky would be attending an away game.

For the time being, though, she was still at school, sitting in the school's newsroom. It was the year's first meeting for student staff members of the school newspaper: *The Black Diamond Daily*. The paper's name was a partial joke, given that the publication came out once every two weeks.

Even so, despite how one boy toward the back of the newsroom was preoccupied with making paper darts out of scratch pieces of paper, being at this meeting was no joking matter for Vicky. Indeed, it was so important to her that she wasn't even distracted by the fact that one of the other students present was Hester, whose glance or two toward Vicky didn't exactly emit waves of goodwill.

Edwin, a senior and the editor of the newspaper, eventually took over the leading of the meeting from the paper's advisory teacher. As Vicky listened, she sat there basking in the personal essence of approval.

The approval of her father.

See, *The Black Diamond Daily* was among a few other newspapers published by high schools located in the city of Port Milestone, USA. However, out of those few school papers, the *Daily* was the only one that came from a community of Black Americans in the city. The community of West Hill.

West Hill formed and began thriving before the turn of the century. Now that the Second World War was over and Americans were spending more finances, the nation looked to be on its way toward an economic boom. Including in Port Milestone's Black Diamond district.

Like so many others in the country, the Phillips family and other West Hill residents had done their part for the war effort during the years of conflict. Vicky's mother had volunteered at the nearest railroad canteen, serving food to soldiers, free of charge. Vicky and her girlfriends had lent their hands to the planting and tending of victory gardens, growing fresh food during the wartime years of food rationing.

Vicky's father had taken a leave of absence from his job as a bank security officer so that he could go down and work at Port Milestone's shipyard, which recruited extra sets of wartime hands. After Roy graduated from high school at the latter end of the war, he joined his father as a shipyard worker. Both father and son were among the millions of Black American men who registered for the military draft during the war, but this father and son ended up in the half of Black registrants who weren't inducted into military service. After the war was over, Roy kept his job at the shipyard, and Vicky's father returned to bank security.

Traditionally, West Hill held three major events down Main Street each year: the Black Diamond Days parade in the summer, the high school's homecoming parade in the fall, and the Christmas Promenade in the winter. But in the year after the war's end, there was one more key procession that took place down Main, held in honor of the nation's Black war veterans—especially because so many of them faced the same racial discrimination in their country after the war that they faced during and before it.

Even if his number had been called in the middle of the conflict, Vicky's father would have then been exempted from the requirement to go serve in the military, being a married man with dependents. Still, it bothered him that so many Black men had been prohibited from fighting on the front lines.

"They thought our people weren't smart or able enough to be real soldiers," he'd remarked on a recent evening in the living room at home. Instead of relaxing in his wingback chair with his ottoman, he'd been pacing the floor, holding one of his older copies of *The West Hill Courier*.

As he slapped the back of his hand against one of the newspaper's articles, he went on in what definitely wasn't one of his jaunty moods. "They made up evaluations to claim that Black men were unfit to fight. That we were only good enough for support or menial military tasks. And some recruiting places? They were turning Black draftees and volunteers away outright. But our men who did make it to combat proved themselves. From our airmen to the men on the ground. Even thousands of Black women in the WAC and all—they proved they were up for the work," he said, referring to the Women's Army Corps and other women's branches of the service.

Vicky's father ran his fingers over more of the paper. "That's why we have to make sure stuff gets written down. Keep records of who we are. So people will know and remember."

He then walked over to where his daughter was seated on the couch, his mood softening. "And now you're about to join the paper at school, hm? Makes me proud, Vicky." He reached down, his fingers giving her forehead a gentle tap. "You're a wise girl. You know?"

A part of Vicky had been basking in that affirmation ever since.

She therefore harbored a sense of clearheaded excitement as she sat in this afternoon meeting for the school newspaper staff. She wasn't, however, overly excited when Edwin named the staff members' various roles. He announced that he'd assigned Vicky Phillips to be the writer of Life Beat. The paper's lifestyle and society column.

After the meeting ended and most of the staff headed out, Vicky approached Edwin for a word at his newsroom desk. "Edwin?"

"Ah! Editor Ed, I am," he acknowledged himself with a big smile, holding out his arms on either side of him, a notepad in one hand and a pencil tucked behind his ear. "I was born for this."

"Right. Editor Ed," Vicky said, restraining some laughter. No one could accuse the young man of being unenthusiastic about the upcoming work, and she had no wish to put a damper on his gusto. So, she kept her attitude light as she mentioned her doubt about the role he'd assigned to her.

Editor Ed dismissed her doubt with a wave of his notepad. "Aw, Life Beat is great. You'll have a ball reporting on stuff like who's dating who around here. Just make sure folks know they're on the record while you're getting the scoop. Don't want to embarrass anybody with your articles. And by the way, off the record—" He lowered his voice. "I thought I heard something about this. Are you dating Chester Cunningham, if you don't mind my asking?"

Much as it had happened the week before, a flattered sensation bubbled up inside Vicky and then fizzled right out of her. *Not interested.* "No," she told Ed.

"Oh? 'No' you don't mind my asking, or 'no' you're not dating him?"

"'No' to both."

"Ah. Good! Wouldn't want anything to get sticky on staff, here." He subtly gestured across the newsroom toward Hester, who'd stayed behind for a talk she was having with the advisory teacher.

Resisting the urge to wonder about any situation she wasn't interested in, Vicky steered her way back on topic. "Yes, well, I'm not sure I'm fashionable enough for writing lifestyle pieces and whatnot."

Ed lifted and dropped a shoulder. "You don't have to be. Just write about people who are."

"Yeah. But dating, and fashion, and, um…recipes. I think I can write news that's more, say—I don't know if 'relevant' is the right word."

"You don't think fashion and recipes are relevant? It wasn't that long ago that we had to ration clothes and food. Of course people want to indulge in fashion and recipes now."

"Oh. Yes. Valid point."

Even as Vicky admitted that validity, she assumed she must have appeared as uncertain as she still felt, because Ed said, "Look, don't worry. When I got the names of the staff, I put a lot of thought into your assignments. There are only two girls on the paper. With Hester coming back this year, she's still a cinch for keeping the advice column in demand. She's so popular that girls will keep writing in to 'Help Me, Hettie!' even if her advice stinks."

Although Vicky was already looking at Ed, she did a double take at him. Which he didn't seem to notice as he went on with, "That leaves you as the choice for Life Beat."

Vicky's next words were more of a vocal reasoning than a question. "Because I'm a girl."

A snicker crackled in Ed's throat. "You think I'd trust Donald to write fashion articles?" He jerked his head toward the boy assigned to report on sports.

Vicky followed the motion of Ed's head, seeing the designated sports reporter now putting his scratch paper darts to the test, finding out how far they could fly across the back of the newsroom.

When Vicky brought her eyes back to Ed, he told her, "We want to keep as many students as possible interested in the paper. And doing something like using a pseudonym in a byline wouldn't keep the writer's identity a secret for long. Not at this school. If students don't think the writer fits the article, they won't read it."

A line formed between Vicky's brows. She tried to reconcile Ed's last statement with his previous indication that she didn't have to be a very fashionable person to write about fashion.

He smiled again. "Just do your best and make me proud, Phillips."

Automatically, she tried to smile back. But, somehow, Ed's bid to her didn't sit quite right. She mentally pulled her father's approval closer about her.

Some time later at home in her room, as Vicky prepared to leave for the football game, she mulled over her newspaper role. There had to be a way she could get her editor to rethink his decision. After all, while she trusted that he'd heard about her being a good student, he couldn't specifically know too much about her writing ability yet.

As she stopped by her dresser to pick up the West Hill High pennant she took along to games, an idea began to stir. If Ed saw that she could write something of quality on a subject he would normally assign to a boy, maybe that would do the trick.

She gave the pennant a pondering wave. It wouldn't even have to be an article meant for publication. Only something to submit for her editor's private perusal, to show him she could do it.

Because this year's first paper would be coming out during Homecoming Week, a written interview with a star football player at West Hill would be sure to go over well with Ed.

And there was one such athlete who had agreed to owe Vicky a favor.

Bingo!

If she wanted to do this in addition to planning and writing an article more in line with her assignment, she'd have to get to her first goal as soon as possible.

At the game that night, Vicky's anticipation regarding her idea added a bonus dash of pep to her cheers for West Hill's football team. As it turned out, their team narrowly lost the game, but their star player made a worthy showing. Fuller of verve and more satisfying to watch than a mere freight truck.

Yet, the following day, Vicky's plan ran into a snag before she even got started. After breakfast, she walked to the grocery with a short shopping list from her mother. A list that included extra flour for some chicken-frying for a church fundraiser. While Vicky was in the process of making her purchases and conversing with the teenaged bag boy about West Hill's varsity game the night before, the bag boy told her, "Willie-with-the-Beard's gonna have to stay home all weekend, though. Brother Brown said."

He referred to Willie's father the way most of the community did. Even for the nonchurchgoers who didn't address anyone else as "brother" or "sister" in a saintly sense, the owner of Bro Brown's was a natural exception.

"He was here earlier," the bag boy explained. "Said Willie's coming down with something. Throat's sore."

That piece of news deflated Vicky. As she returned home with a bag of groceries, she considered her plan to now be out of the question.

But then her thoughts took a different tack.

THE NEXT DAY AFTER her family's morning at West Hill First Baptist Church, Vicky set aside the Sunday suit and hat she'd donned for service, and she put on a more comfortable skirt, blouse, and a pair of loafers. She then took a walk over to the Browns' house, a canvas bag of supplies hanging from her arm.

"Hello, Brother Brown," she greeted Willie's father when he answered the front door.

"Well, well! Miss Vicky," he returned her greeting with a smile. "You eat up my burgers every other week, but it's been a while since you rang our bell over here."

"Yes, it has," she agreed, neither she nor Brother Brown expressly mentioning the years before his wife's passing.

"Word around town is they've got a nickname for you now, young lady. For getting perfect marks in school."

That detail tickled and slightly embarrassed Vicky at the same time. "You've heard that about me?"

"Sure have. Only surprise is that The Brain ain't jumped straight to college yet. But where are my manners? Come on in." Once Vicky was inside, Brother Brown closed the door and gestured further into the living room, where a matronly woman was sitting in an armchair, sleeping. "You know Miss Mavis. Still comes in to help with the housekeeping."

Having not expected to see Miss Mavis in slumber, Vicky brought a cautious hand up to her lips. But Brother Brown said, "Don't worry. Can't hardly nothing wake her up from her Sabbath snooze. So, what brings you by?"

Bringing her eyes back from Miss Mavis, Vicky patted her bag. "I heard about Willie. Thought he could use something for his throat."

Before Brother Brown could reply to that, the muffled thump of descending footsteps sounded on the stairway right off of the living room, and Willie appeared.

Appeared in a blue bathrobe wrapped over striped pajamas.

Vicky's cheeks heated as Brother Brown all but boomed out with a grin, "Hey, Willie. Dr. Vicky here's making a house call."

Vicky's foot took an involuntary hint of a step back. "I should have phoned first," she mumbled, her eyes flitting over Willie and then up toward the ceiling. Or somewhere.

The quiet voice that came to Vicky's ears was a mix of air and a crackling sheet of sandpaper. "Aw, don't be shy about the pj's." At that, she brought her eyes back down to find the light of laughter in Willie's as he told her, "Nothing better than the clothes you open Christmas presents in. Huh?"

A chortle had no choice but to bounce clear up from Vicky's middle. She gave in to the delight of it. "Then in that case, Merry Christmas. I've come bearing my big red bag." Even though her canvas bag was beige, she made a show of pointing it out. "If I could use a pot, please?"

Willie turned questioning eyes on his father, who only motioned for him to go on ahead. So, Willie nodded the way forward. "Oh, yeah. Come on to the kitchen."

In the kitchen, as Willie took out a pot and utensils at Vicky's request, she set her bag in a chair at the round kitchen table and moved to the sink to wash her hands. She was digging her needed supplies out of her bag when Willie asked, "So...what's happening?"

Vicky looked up to see him hovering between the stove and the table, looking lost in his own kitchen.

She asked him, "Have you had any lemons and honey? Because I'm making some."

It took a second for that piece of information to register. "Lemons and honey?" Willie asked. "For me?"

"Mm hm. For your throat."

When he only stood there a moment longer, Vicky nodded toward the table as she headed for the counter and the cutting board with her lemons. "It's all right. Have a seat," she bid Willie. As he slowly obeyed, she caught a glimpse of Brother Brown grinning past the kitchen doorway and disappearing, the muffled beat of his ascending footsteps sounding on the stairway.

Once Vicky had a kettle of water heating on the stove and got her lemon slicing started, she asked Willie, "How're you feeling?"

His grunt had more air than an actual grunt in it. "I sound worse than I feel. I wasn't that sick yesterday either. But, well, my dad worries."

That comment made Vicky pause to look at Willie. There was something sensitive in the smile he allowed. It seemed he briefly lowered his already limited voice on purpose to say, "I'm the only boy he's got."

Again, the thought of Willie's late mother drifted through the place. Vicky allowed a small smile as well, only able to imagine life as an only child with but one remaining parent.

After a minute, Willie shifted the conversation, asking, "Was it a good week at school for you?"

Vicky answered in the affirmative as she got back to her preparations, adding, "I joined the school newspaper. Editor Ed assigned me to the Life Beat column, but I'm not sure I'm with-it enough for that. I don't keep up with the times too well, as far as doing all the popular things folks do. But I want to be a journalist, so I need some newspaper practice."

"A journalist? You mean a real one?"

"Yes. After college." When Vicky glanced at Willie, his interested look encouraged her to share some more. "The news has always been important in my family, and writing is important to me. So I started wanting to write the news. Maybe I'll write books too, someday. I don't know. But newspapers are what so many people read every day. Including some people who may not read that many books—they still look through the papers. Talk about what's in them." Even more than parental approval, personal hope fed into her next words. "I want to be a part of informing people. Writing what they'll read and talk about."

She kept busy with her task at the cutting board and the stove, and it wasn't too long before she had the lemons and honey drink ready to pour from the pot and into a mug. When she placed the warm mug on the table before Willie, he murmured his thanks with a clear share of amazement. As if he couldn't quite believe she'd done it.

Vicky made a cup of warm water with lemon for herself so that Willie wouldn't be the only one drinking something. She walked around to take the seat on his left, and after they'd each had sips from their cups, Willie wagged a thoughtful finger at her.

"You know, come to think of it," he said, "it's not hard to see you being a journalist. A good one. With a reporter hat. With one of those little papers sticking up out of it."

A smile spread over Vicky's face. "A press pass?"

"If that's what they're called, yeah."

"And you think I'd be good?"

"Sure! You're already finding a way to work toward it. At school. And your grades prove you work hard." Willie nodded at her. "It'll be good for you, knowing what your focus is in college."

"Well. Thank you. For saying so." Because her measure of motivation shot up in such an elated way, Vicky took her time with another sip of her water. Once she'd collected herself, she asked Willie, "Are you planning on college?"

"Yup." He drank more from his mug and cleared his hoarse throat. "I don't catch on to everything in school, though. Memorizing dates and formulas. Or figuring out Shakespeare. But by the time I'm all done with a class, I come out knowing at least some stuff I didn't know before. That's good, right?"

It took Vicky a second to realize Willie was actually asking her. She nodded her agreement, and he seemed satisfied with it.

"So, yeah," he said, "I'm planning on college. Will see how much I can learn. Football will get me there."

That declaration piqued Vicky's curiosity. "Yeah?"

Willie took a pause from drinking to study her. Apparently, he was now the one who needed to see if she was truly asking him before he went on. "Sports are turning into a bigger deal at colleges. Football especially. Schools want to bring in talent, and my name's out there. Not quite sure where I'll go yet. But me and my dad got some plans started."

"I see. Good for you, Willie. That sounds great."

"Does it, to you? I know that going to school for football isn't the same as..." He gestured toward Vicky with one hand.

His unfinished comparison gave Vicky an awkward feeling, but she moved past it easily enough, saying, "See, though? That's the thing about college. Everybody there doesn't have to focus on the same stuff. Like you said, we learn what we can in class. But spending years and years burying your nose in more formulas? Give the real formula fanatics a hankie and leave them to it."

It pleased Vicky that her joke made Willie laugh. Or wheeze. Whichever he was doing at the moment.

When his laugh-wheezing subsided, she said, "Besides, it isn't as though football isn't important."

Willie had lifted his mug for another sip, but he stopped short, putting the mug back down, his eyes blinking a few surprised times at Vicky.

She hurried on to explain. "That is, we need sports and entertainment, don't we? Even during the war, they sent all those performers overseas. A way to keep the troops entertained. And to keep morale up. It was important. I'm not even the biggest sports fan around, but I started going to football and basketball games because my friends do. And guess what, doggone it?"

An additional spark of surprise shone through Willie's now twinkling eyes. "What?"

"Going to games is fun! Even for a brainy book-eater like me. Go figure."

That brought another bout of laugh-wheezing from Willie, although the bout was shorter and even airier this time. One of his elbows slid its way onto the table.

Vicky chuckled herself, and then she sobered, saying, "Things like football… It brings people together. Keeps our spirits up." She gave the table a decided pat near Willie. "We need that."

She noticed it then. It wasn't only that Willie had his elbow on the table. He'd raised a fist for the side of his face to lean against as he stared at Vicky, the essence of laughter lingering in his…somewhat drowsy look? Somewhat moonstruck?

Vicky's cheeks were in danger of heating again.

Her mind reached for a diversion, finding one in the form of Willie's mug. She signaled for him to get back to his drink and inquired of him, "What about you? For after college, I mean."

Willie sat up and drained the rest that he could from his mug before answering. "If I'm good enough, it'd be something to be a football player. A professional one. And the major league is integrated now. Eventually, though, I want to work with my dad."

As she picked up her cup to finish her water, Vicky added deliberate nonchalance to her voice. "Oh, your dad plays football too?"

Willie's shoulders gave a small bounce of humor, but his answer was, "I want to help run the business. Bro Brown's. Probably take it over someday. Pass it on to my own son. Or daughter."

Vicky's eyebrows rose. She was slow in setting her cup back down as she reflected aloud, "Hm. A real family business."

"Yup. The best business, if you ask me. And not just 'cause the grub is good. It's a good spot for the neighborhood. The people." Willie fell silent for a time, studying Vicky some more, then he beckoned her with the motion of his head. "Come here."

He stood up from the table, and Vicky did the same with interest, following him out of the kitchen and into the living room. The two of them made their quiet way past the snoozing Miss Mavis, and they approached a record player cabinet near one corner of the room.

As Willie lifted the top of the cabinet to reveal the player, he whispered, "You should see my dad when he gets riled up, talking about most radio stations refusing to play race music. Especially the blues. A lot of folks just listening to the radio—they wouldn't know about a lot of the Black singers and musicians around. But my dad has his record player so he can choose his own mix of music to buy. Whether it's on the radio or not." Willie jerked a thumb to one side. "That's the main reason he got the jukebox for Bro Brown's. Everybody who comes in there can hear a good mix of records."

Vicky's head moved pensively up and down. Venturing to open one of the cabinet's doors, she took a peek at the ample collection of records stored inside as Willie told her, "And more records upstairs."

Vicky looked up at Willie, her mood still reflective. Appreciative. "Music brings people together too," she whispered.

"Yeah. Exactly. Then combine that with good grub? Man!" Willie's head shook with his own appreciation. "It's something, Vicky."

She barely moved her eyes from him as she closed the cabinet door. *Something.* A nonspecific word with so much behind it in this case, positively emanating from Willie. Vicky simply stood there sensing it, for a while.

Yes. Really something.

Nonetheless, she'd been here at the Browns' house for about as long as she'd intended to be. She would have to be on her way back home soon, a fact probably made plain by the reluctant glance she took toward the front door.

Willie almost glanced that way when she did. But he stopped and smiled at her instead, his voice still at the physical level of air only. "Thanks for honey..." His words trailed off, his expression of thanks remaining as it was for a beat or two.

A beat or two that had Vicky wondering if her knees were, perhaps, getting wobbly.

Willie then gave a little start and a hard blink, his smile going lopsided. "For the lemons and honey," he corrected himself.

Vicky nodded, waving toward the kitchen. "I should clean up my mess in there."

"Oh, no, I'll take care of it. This is your first time here in forever, and you already went to work at the stove. Miss Mavis would pop me if she found out I had a guest washing dishes." Willie brought a hand back and swatted it past his ear, bobbling his head at the imaginary pop. "Really, though, I'm glad about the, um, house call. Dr. Vicky."

A titter skittered out of her. "Some doctor I am. I've had you talking so much, you might lose the rest of your voice anyway."

Willie gave his head one faint shake. "If I do, it was worth it."

Oh! My. Vicky resisted the impulse to bring a hand up to her cheek. Her first time being here in forever, and she didn't recall any of her previous visits making her this warm, back then. Not even after running around outside.

It wasn't until Vicky was back at home, having a minute alone with her canvas bag, that she finally pulled out the last of the supplies she'd taken along on her visit. A pencil, and a notepad with a few prewritten questions scrawled down on it.

Questions she'd left unasked.

When Willie let her know that he actually wasn't feeling too sick? That should have been her open door to tell him about the rest of the plan she had in mind and to carry the plan out. Right?

Yet, here Vicky was, having spent a good portion of the afternoon talking with her school's star football player in advance of Homecoming Week, and she hadn't asked him for anything to put on the record.

She now breathed a sigh, a delicate smile wandering along her lips as she put her pencil and notepad away.

Chapter Four

THE FOLLOWING TUESDAY at school, Vicky was standing at her open locker in a bustling hallway. Lunch hour had just started. While she was stowing away the schoolbooks she'd already used that day, she heard someone call her name through the bustle.

She looked up to see Willie headed in her direction. He eased his path through other students, making quick work of returning a few greetings he received along the way. Once he reached Vicky, he grinned at her over a short stack of schoolbooks he was holding up. "Hey."

"Hello there." Vicky's eyes flew over the letterman jacket Willie happened to be wearing today, with their school's prominent initials "WH" displayed on the front left. She also gave his face a look-over. "How're you feeling today?"

"Solid." He nodded down at his stack of books. "I brought this for you."

On top of the book stack was something smaller, wrapped in wax paper. Vicky tentatively reached for it, only picking it up from the stack after Willie gave her another encouraging nod. Before she could ask what it was, he announced, "It's a peanut butter and jelly sandwich. Ever had one before?"

A curious smile came to Vicky's face. "Um, I've had peanut butter sandwiches. Haven't had one with jelly."

"Good! Then I'm helping you keep up with the times. A little, anyway. Our soldiers ate a lot of those during the war. Now folks are eating 'em all over the place." Willie was still holding up his stack of schoolbooks like a tray. "I made that with a lot of peanut butter. A lot of grape jelly too. So the bread wouldn't soak it all up before I got it to you."

"Is that right?" An unfamiliar impression came to Vicky, though she was technically aware that it wasn't anything new for a teenaged boy to give a teenaged girl a gift.

She'd heard of boys bringing corsages to their dates for dances. Events that Vicky didn't attend. She'd been told that some boys gave girls their ID bracelets. A serious gift category that Vicky wouldn't warrant expecting from any boy at this stage of her life experience.

She couldn't say she'd ever particularly heard of a teenaged boy giving a teenaged girl a sandwich.

Maybe if she were more studied in the area of advice and society columns, she'd have a better idea of precisely how she was supposed to view such an offering. She knew of no specific rule that her emotions were supposed to follow, here. So, in this situation, what came naturally to Vicky simply happened.

Something inside of her melted.

Her head dipped as a warm laugh escaped her over this gift meant to help her keep up with the times. A little, anyway.

"You were listening," she observed to Willie, her fingers careful not to squish the sandwich. No telling if "a lot" of peanut butter and jelly meant that the sandwich could burst at any moment. "Thank you, Willie."

"Thank *you*. I guess I haven't really evened the score yet." When Vicky only gave him a puzzled look, Willie said, "I knock you over at Bro Brown's. I leave there owing you. Then you hear I'm sick, you come over to see me, and you feed me honey." He inclined his head somewhat closer to her over his books. "Score ain't even yet."

Oh. Wow. For all of Vicky's melting, she couldn't avoid the mental pang that disrupted her thoughts. She murmured, "We don't have to keep score." She took a second before drawing a deep breath. "Willie, when I came over, I was going to try to get an interview with you. For—for the school paper." Thrown by the faltering of her own voice, she had to pause.

Willie's schoolbooks gradually lowered.

"Well," Vicky went on, "not for the paper, but to show Editor Ed. So he'd see I could write something like that."

Once Vicky finished that confession, Willie repositioned his books, holding them in one hand down against his side. While half a smile remained on his face, more than half of what had been behind it seemed to wane. His reply was a quiet one. "You didn't come over just to doctor me, then."

Vicky gave something that fell in between a nod and a shrug as she took care in pointing out, "Well, letting me have an interview would have been a favor. You know?"

Willie's head shifted at an angle. In response to her angle.

Beginning to feel at a loss for words, Vicky searched that much harder for them. "So I planned on asking you. But then I

got there, and you were in your pajamas. Looking comfy and...I
don't know. Homey." The remainder of Willie's smile appeared
amused by that, if also a bit sheepish, as she continued. "And
we were there in the kitchen. Just, you know. Sitting there.
Talking." One of Vicky's thumbs rubbed over the sandwich in
her hands. "It was nice."

As she stood there praying he'd understand, Willie's jaw
moved around, almost as if to literally chew on her
explanation. His look was cautious as he asked, "So...it wasn't
just an interview?"

Vicky shook her head. "It wasn't an interview at all. It was
just us."

Willie's eyes grew at the reference to "us." He looked
downward, shuffling his feet, the ball of one foot twisting back
and forth against the floor before he lifted his gaze back to
Vicky. He wasn't smiling anymore. "Well, then. I don't care
what you say." A glisten came to his eyes, light mischief in his
low voice. "I still owe you."

Vicky stared at him, and after a delay, a chortle of relief
floated from her. She wouldn't try to get an interview from him
again; the thought of it had spoiled for her. All the same, she
was relieved.

Now, her laugh seemed to free up space for a nervous
chuckle from Willie. Why his chuckle would be a nervous one,
she couldn't tell. It was accompanied by his free hand reaching
up to rub along the back of his neck.

He opened his mouth again, right on the verge of—

"Vicky!"

She froze at the sound of Berta's voice, calling out behind
her.

After that, the moment got away from Vicky. Later on, she would vaguely remember Willie smiling a sudden goodbye at her and her friends, since both Berta and Evie approached her as Willie was taking his leave.

Vicky, watching him disappear back down the hall, only partially heard from her side, "Vick? Something up with you and Willie-with-the-Beard?"

In a daze, Vicky turned to her girlfriends, her gift in wax paper still cradled in her hands. Her partial hearing had been enough to prompt her amazed whisper that followed. "Willie, he... He made me a sandwich."

Berta's and Evie's mouths sank open simultaneously. "Say again?" Evie chirped.

Questions. Vicky's friends were going to have more questions. And in contrast to the last Saturday of summer break, when Vicky had kept the news of an, um, incident all to herself—today she was raring to spill.

She spun around to finish up in her locker, determined that she would go spill as much as she could to her friends over lunch.

Granted, afterward, she wouldn't be able to say that she spilled absolutely everything. Somehow, the afternoon she'd spent with Willie felt too special to share every detail of it. Also, she didn't eat her peanut butter and jelly sandwich for lunch. It was too special to be scarfed down in a distracted hurry while she was trying to catch Berta and Evie up on everything. Even if it wasn't absolutely everything.

Instead, Vicky saved her sandwich for a leisurely afterschool snack at home in the kitchen. She enjoyed it with a glass of milk and a couple of chapters of a novel before homework.

Mmm. It might as well have been ambrosia on bread. For a variety of reasons, this gift of a snack surpassed all of the plain peanut butter she'd ever eaten.

She took a pause from her novel, slowly chewing. Picturing the giver of this gift. How he'd grinned as he'd given it to her. Standing there with his stack of schoolbooks. Wearing his letterman jacket.

Vicky sat up straighter at the kitchen table.

Homecoming festivities next week. West Hill High School spirit. Team pride. Lettermen walking around campus in their lettermen's wear.

Fashion!

She could do some research to write a short background on the history of letterman sweaters and jackets. Making a stop the next day at the school library and possibly the public library should take care of that. She could tie the general background into West Hill's own letterman tradition and homecoming honors. There was likely a related photograph or illustration on file at school to print or reprint for this upcoming edition of the *Daily.*

When Vicky typed up her fashion article on a school newsroom typewriter that Thursday, she finished it off with: "So, for all that these fellows do to boost our morale after the long, hard weeks of classes, let's be sure to return the favor. We don't even have to wait until after the Friday-night wins. When you see the back of one or another of our athletes passing by in their lettermen's garb, make your appreciation known and kindly pat that back!"

Turning the article in to Editor Ed made her the first to do so.

"Hey," he said after he read her piece on the spot. "Nice theme for Homecoming Week. I bet some of the guys might use it as a call for a varsity slap-fest—'See a letterman, slap his back! Or the back of his head!'—but I think folks in general will get the spirit of it."

Vicky laughed her thanks, not sure if Ed was joking about the slap-fest or not. Either way, her first piece for the paper was an adequate effort, she reasoned. Its tie to football might be the next best thing to the first idea she'd had. Even if carrying out her first idea wouldn't have been for publication.

Yet, Vicky pondered as she gathered her belongings and left the newsroom for home: She wouldn't want this sentiment to become a regular thing, would she? To feel as though her byline would be printed on an article that was only the "next best" idea she'd had?

Hmm...

At any rate, her editor liked the article. While it made her anxious to imagine how more of her fellow students might or might not react to her column, she looked forward to seeing her byline in print.

ON A DIFFERENT NOTE, it turned out that something else involving Vicky would soon spread through much of the school to meet with reactions from her fellow students.

The next afternoon, classes let out with their normal bonus degree of Friday excitement. Vicky would be going to another away game for the varsity football team, and she wanted to finish her homework beforehand, if she could.

When she exited through the school's front doors to head for home, a small group of boys stood off to the side of the crowd on the portico, which wasn't unusual. But before Vicky could get to the front steps, the boy in the center of that group pushed off of the column he'd been leaning against and stepped into Vicky's path.

She came to an abrupt stop, clutching her book bag hanging from her shoulder, nearly running into the boy before she stepped back. "Oh. Um, hi, Chester."

Sunlight shining through the portico columns gleamed on the side of Chester Cunningham's impeccably brushed and oiled hair. A wavy hairdo as lustrous as that of a suave jazz singer ready to perform onstage in a ritzy establishment.

In a relaxed posture with his hands in the pockets of his sharp trousers, Chester smiled at Vicky. "Well, if it isn't the beautiful Brain!" he hailed her. In a loud voice.

Loud enough to draw the attention of other students milling around the portico and on the steps. Everyone else's chatter and activity out there didn't come to a complete stop, but even without looking, Vicky could sense multiple pairs of eyes turning her way.

The richest and arguably finest boy in Black Diamond had paid Vicky a personal compliment. In public. An occurrence that would definitely merit a swooning response from a girl.

Yet, in the face of so personal and sudden a compliment, out here in public, Vicky's instincts skipped succumbing to a swoon. Her mind reached for a comic deflection instead.

"Oh, we've seen pictures of the human brain in science class," she replied to Chester, circling a finger near her face. "Is that what I look like?"

He gave a good-humored chuckle. "Ha! You're funny." He brought his hands out of his pockets, slapping them together. "So, Vicky! You. Me. The homecoming dance. What do you say?" His palms slid against each other in an easy, anticipatory rub. "We'll be chauffeured by my father's driver for the night."

Oh, mercy.

That Berta and Evie. The two of them had been so sure that this was coming. Vicky, on the other hand, had expressed suspicion and an otherwise lack of interest over it, doing nothing to plan ahead for this.

Hence, the question that slid out next wasn't her most intentional. Or her most audible. "Me? Why?" she wanted to know.

Despite her mumbly volume, Chester must have heard her just fine. Whether or not he fully understood what he heard was another matter, but his shoulders came up in a doubtless gesture. His hands spread out, his tone as light and smooth as whipped butter as he answered, "Because I'm asking you, beautiful."

Vicky stood there, blinking at him.

Ah. Yes. After hailing her at an audience-grabbing decibel, he was asking her. Perhaps, being so generous as to ask this girl he hardly ever talked to—her brainy status and newly declared beauty notwithstanding.

All at once, more than before, whatever actual reasons Chester Cunningham might have for asking Vicky Phillips to the upcoming dance didn't matter.

"No, thank you," she told him.

A trace of disbelief altered the tilt of Chester's smile. "What?" he asked on a gust of laughter, quick and short.

"No, thank you, Chester." Vicky gave him a small smile in return as she stepped out of his way. "You have a good weekend, all right?"

The multiple pairs of watching eyes out there had multiplied further. Vicky did her best not to let her own eyes run directly into any of them, knowing that the news (more accurately, rumors) about this would start spreading behind her before she even made it down the street. She descended the front steps of the building, looking over at the school's clock tower, wanting to appear to be in a hurry to get home.

Not that she hadn't already been in a hurry to get home. She wanted to finish her homework before the football game, of course.

Thankfully, after that unusual dance invitation, the Homecoming Week that followed was a normal one for Vicky.

Mostly normal, anyhow.

The week included her usual presence with her girlfriends at the homecoming parade down Main Street and their varsity football team's first home game of the season at West Hill Memorial Field. Vicky's parents went to the game as well. As Roy also attended the game with a few of his own friends, the Phillips family was represented in three different parts of the stands full of West Hill High students, past and present.

Now, as far as Vicky was concerned, what was new about Homecoming Week this year?

Her byline in *The Black Diamond Daily*, for one. All things considered, she was proud to see it.

She remained proud even as Editor Ed proved to have a share of accurate foresight in regard to the guys at their school. The slap-fest he'd predicted did manifest in a few of the school's hallways. Not in too rampant a manner, though, and the targeted lettermen laughingly gave as good as they got.

Also, it hadn't occurred to Vicky that she would notice lettermen passing by more than she usually did, as she couldn't encourage her fellow students to do something she wasn't going to do herself. That Friday at school, she wound up going out of her way to pat the shoulders of a few lettermen in this hallway or that, giving them a hearty "Good luck!" for good measure. (Yes, she opted to go for their shoulders rather than their backs, so that she could make eye contact first. She didn't want to attempt any back-patting from behind that could initially be mistaken for participation in the slap-fest.)

Added to that, Vicky hadn't supposed how it would feel to receive the appreciation of several lettermen as she wished them luck, even if it was but in passing.

"Yeah, thanks, Vicky!"

"Aw, The Brain speaks. Thank you!"

"'Preciate it, Vicky! I'd ask you to the dance if I didn't already have a date. Heard you gave Chester Cunningham a big fat 'no way'—"

"Man, leave her alone. Don't listen to him, Vicky. And thanks!"

Given that all of this took place but in passing, she hadn't the chance to explain to the lettermen that her simple answer to Chester Cunningham's dance invitation had been neither big nor fat.

One other new experience for her happened at the homecoming game that night. When West Hill's star football player scored his second touchdown of the game, he turned and spotted Vicky in the stands and extended his arm in her direction, pointing the football at her.

That is, she imagined he pointed the football at her. Berta and Evie were a lot more certain about it than she was.

"What's to doubt, Vicky?" Berta asked her. "It's obvious he was pointing at you. Wouldn't have any reason to be pointing at me or Evie. Or Howard. Right, Howard?" she asked her boyfriend sitting on her other side.

Howard slid his arm around Berta's shoulders, providing his girlfriend with a joking answer to it all. "Yeah, he better not be pointing at you, Birdie."

That answer was no help to Vicky, but it made little difference. Her cheering down at their team's star player and waving her pennant at him were appropriate actions no matter who he'd pointed at.

Even so, Homecoming Week normality resumed for Vicky on the day after. Saturday evening. For the third year in a row, her girlfriends attended the homecoming dance with their dates and plenty of other members of the student body, and Vicky stayed home.

Chapter Five

THE MONDAY FOLLOWING the week of homecoming festivities was a comedown for many of West Hill High's students. As for Vicky, she welcomed Mondays, and Mondays welcomed her. She was bright-eyed and ready to work as she sat in English class that morning.

Her teacher was announcing the start of a study on narrative poetry, telling the class, "As a part of this study, you'll each be working with a partner for a few weeks to co-write a narrative poem. You'll look for more examples of narrative poetry together and get an idea of the kind of story you wish to tell through your piece. We'll discuss poem lengths a bit later, but the main requirement will be that the poem you write must tell a complete story. Now, I'll give you all a few minutes to go around the room and choose a partner."

A slight slump came to Vicky's shoulders. Partnering into pairs or groups wasn't her favorite way to work at school. Not when it meant being graded as a group on an assignment. Because Vicky was unwilling to let group work lower her grades, the responsibility of making sure her groups' assignments would receive high marks largely fell on her, much of the time. It didn't help that other students seemed to think it was only natural for The Brain of West Hill High to go to extra lengths on her own. Extra lengths that her partners wouldn't have realized were necessary for their joint work. They wouldn't have realized, or sometimes they wouldn't have cared either way.

Hence, Vicky didn't jump out of her seat when other classmates of hers did in English class that morning, the quickest students popping around to pair up with their friends.

But it was only a matter of seconds before the emptied desk on Vicky's right was claimed by a boy who hurried over with his schoolbooks and slid into the seat. He turned his golden brown, freckled face to Vicky with an excited smile. "Hello! Don't know if you know me, but I'm Thomas. My first year at this school. Would you like to be my partner?"

Vicky looked down in surprise at the hand of greeting Thomas thrust out across the aisle. She reached to shake hands with him, beginning to introduce herself.

"Oh, I know who you are, Vicky," Thomas cut off her introduction, giving her hand a lively pump and letting it go. "I've heard all about The Brain. So I'm glad I got to you first. To be honest, I normally don't care to work with partners. I wind up doing most of the work that way. My partners tend to think I'm a free ride to an A plus. But I'm guessing you're the type who'll want to work as hard as I do, hopefully?"

Vicky's shoulders had lifted from their slump. Although Thomas's direct comments had taken her off guard, they were refreshing comments to hear. She found herself smiling back at him, saying, "Actually, it sounds to me like you're the type who'll want to work as hard as *I* do."

Thomas laughed. "Ah, music to my ears. So that's a 'yes' to being partners, then?"

"Yes, that's a 'yes.'"

"Yes!" Thomas gave one fist a small pump of triumph, and Vicky laughed this time.

Their teacher soon called everyone back to order, and Thomas remained at the desk near Vicky's. At the end of class, he turned to her again, asking the soonest day she'd be available to meet him at the public library. "The book selection's better there than the school library," he said, "and I'd like to get our poetry hunting started right away. If that's all right."

There, now, was music to Vicky's ears. No procrastination from Thomas about getting down to business. Without hesitation, she agreed to meet him at the public library after school, setting a time that would allow each of them to stop at home first.

However, Vicky did run into some hesitation later that day, when she showed up at the library at the appointed hour. Thomas was waiting outside of the building's entrance, looking down the street in the opposite direction from Vicky. It was evident that he'd used his time to make a stop at someplace other than his home, what with the small bouquet of pink carnations he held in his hands.

Vicky spoke up to get his attention as she approached him. "Hello..."

After he visibly startled, Thomas turned around. "Ah! You're here. On time too. Great! These are for you." He thrust the bouquet toward her.

"They are?" Vicky didn't reach for his offering, an uncertain smile coming to her face. "Um, why?"

Thomas looked a tad confused by the question. "Why?" He glanced toward the library entrance behind him. "Well, I asked you here."

"Yes." Vicky's head moved slowly up and down. "For a class assignment," she carefully stated.

Thomas drew the bouquet back a degree. "They're too much?" His eyes dropped to the carnations for a second. "I don't mean them as too much, just as a thank-you for being my partner." An abashed smile tugged on his mouth. "First time I've ever been glad about having someone to share homework with."

In the untimely spirit of inconvenience, Vicky caught a visual of Evie at Bro Brown's, clasping her hands together, rhapsodizing about doves and violins and Miss Tatum the librarian telling the violins to hush up while a prince and princess mooned at each other over their history notes and math problems.

Thomas could have no way of knowing that Vicky's embarrassed but affectionate trickle of laughter had little to do with him, specifically. The sound of her laugh seemed to give him a new hint of hope.

"Please," he said, holding the bouquet closer to her again. "They're for you."

With a light, yielding sigh, Vicky finally accepted the flowers, murmuring a word of thanks.

Thomas grinned and wasted no more time. He made haste to go open one of the library doors, holding it so that Vicky could walk in ahead of him. A short time later, while the two of them browsed among the library's poetry shelves, Thomas took it upon himself to carry the books that he and Vicky selected. When they'd finished their browsing and chose a table for their work, Thomas pulled out Vicky's chair for her before taking his own seat.

Their poetry reading and discussion on language and narrative moved right along from there. Quietly, of course, so as not to trouble the ears of Miss Tatum or any others in the library. Vicky became so engrossed in the study session itself that she took no conscious notice of how comfortable a session it was.

She didn't feel a tinge of uncertainty again until she got back home, entering the living room. Her mother, who was on her way to the kitchen, stopped to stare at the small bundle of pink in her daughter's hands.

"Victoria? I thought you went out to the library."

"Mm? I did." Vicky held up the bouquet in a noncommittal fashion. "My study partner wanted to thank me. For being his partner."

"Study partner? Your study partner who?"

"Thomas. A new boy. At school."

"Hm. I see." Vicky's mother's movement was unrushed as she folded her arms, lifting her brows over subtle twinkles in her eyes. "So. This appointment to go study with Thomas the new boy from school. Did it happen to be, dare I say, a date?"

Vicky's own eyes widened. "No..." she began, but then found that she had to think it over. She looked down at her carnations before meeting her mother's gaze again.

As Vicky's mouth slanted with unsure amusement, she mused aloud, "It wasn't like that. But, um, maybe he planned on turning it into something like that? Sort of?"

IT MUST HAVE BEEN A week for the unexpected.

When Vicky arrived at school the following morning, she spotted part of an envelope peeking out of the slit at the bottom of her locker. She went and pulled out the envelope, opening it to read the note inside:

Dear Lemons and Honey Girl, Bookworm, and Journalist-to-be,
Miss Mavis said it would be nicer if I write this to you instead of
calling you about it. I don't know much about fancy invitations.
I'm having people over at the house on Saturday night to listen to
records. Can you come? You can ask some of your friends to come
too. Maybe two or three people with you would be fine. We won't
run out of food.
My dad will be home, so your parents don't have to worry that it
will be a wild party. You don't have to wear your Sunday best,
but I promise I'll be more dressed up than my pajamas.

Vicky didn't make it to the additional details at the end of the note before she started laughing to herself. Joy and jitters began swelling up in competing measures within her.

She needed Berta and Evie. Needed them to share her jubilation but also to help calm her down. No, Vicky didn't receive party invitations from boys every day, but she hadn't any doubt that she wanted to go to Willie's on Saturday. Her

girlfriends would know how to keep her from bringing more jitters with her than necessary.

Oh, if only she didn't have to wait all the way until lunch hour to spill the latest and to make sure her friends would want to go to Willie's too.

Granted, even with the positive responses that she did end up receiving from Berta and Evie that day at lunch, there was still the question of obtaining parental permission. Vicky got right to it that evening at home, as her family sat around the dinner table.

They'd barely finished saying grace over their meal before Vicky plunged in. "There's a little party I want to go to this Saturday night. That is, I guess it'll be a party. With records and food."

"A party where?" Vicky's mother was swift to ask, somehow making her daughter suspect that her mother suspected it had something to do with a certain library outing and pink carnations.

Vicky was eager to clarify that that wasn't the case. "Over at the Browns' house. Willie-with-the—" The threat of a laugh in her throat interrupted her, but she succeeded in swallowing it. "Willie Brown invited me."

"No kiddin'," Vicky's father blatantly commented rather than asked as he cut into the meat on his plate.

When Vicky gave her father a quizzical look, Roy piped up to tell her, "We all saw it, Vicky."

Vicky turned her look on her brother. "Saw what?"

"At the homecoming game. When Willie pointed at you in the stands." Roy tapped a finger underneath one of his eyes. "From what I've seen, Willie usually waves up at his dad after his first touchdown and leaves it at that. But this time, when he scores another touchdown, he turns around and points the ball up at you." Roy's eyebrows bounced a couple of deliberate times. "Now, why in the world would he do that?"

Vicky's mouth wandered open some seconds before she was ready to reply. "Maybe because I went to see him the other week. When he was sick."

In reaction to that particular piece of information, Vicky's father's tone turned genuinely curious. "Oh, yeah?" But his attitude switched right back. "And you nursed him back to health—is that it?"

Vicky shrugged. "He wasn't too sick, really. But I made him something to drink. For his throat."

The look that Vicky's mother cast on her was one of surprise, but with a saucy quality to it as she asked, "Did you now?"

Before Vicky could answer, Roy started humming the tune of "I Love You Truly," his voice making a nasally impression of a muted horn. As if he thought he was Erskine Hawkins.

A reminiscent smile came to Vicky's mother's lips as she reflected to her daughter, "Back when I used to go see Sister Brown, I remember how you and Willie would go run around outside. Then you'd come running back inside. Running in and out. Giggling and hollering." She shook her head. "The both of you would look a mess by the end of all that ruckus, and that's the truth."

"No runnin' around," a deep-voiced order buzzed into the discussion.

With a wrinkling forehead, Vicky turned toward the order's issuer. "Dad?"

Her father speared a chunk of potato onto his fork. "You can go out and, you know—see a boy sometimes. Sure." He pointed a firm finger at his daughter. "But no runnin' around."

Vicky lifted an innocent hand, laughter scuttling over the edges of her reply. "I don't want to run around. I just want to go to the Browns' on Saturday night. Brother Brown will be there, looking out."

"No running in and out nowhere. And no lookin' a mess either. Or whatever young folks are up to these days."

Vicky dropped her head with a snort of restrained hilarity.

Meanwhile, horn-humming must have been an insufficient means for Roy to get his message across. He broke into the song's lyrics in a warbly voice and a higher octave than his natural one, expressing how truly the singer—a lady, apparently—loved her dear.

Vicky snapped her head around to Roy. "Wait. You seriously know the words to that?"

Vicky's father snickered. "He knows them because of that Nella Johnson up the road, I bet."

Roy's song paused as he brought a hand up to his chest. "Hey. I'm not the subject of this conversation." His singing recommenced.

"Yes," Vicky's mother's voice smoothed its way over to her daughter, alongside the singing. "You can go to the party on Saturday. Your father or I will drive you over and pick you up." She then gave her son a pointed look. "Or your brother will."

Roy's warbling cut out. "I have a date that night."

His father grinned across the table at him. "A date to go serenade Nella? Boy, you better sound better than that when you get there."

Roy gave a long blink of dignity before he tucked into his plate, cutting a bite of his meat without a word. With only hushed, perhaps slightly humbled, humming. Still warbly.

Vicky released a big sigh. More like a gust of glee. "Thanks, Mom," she said to put ending punctuation on that phase of their dinner.

As it turned out, another gust on Vicky's part happened in reverse later that week, when she showed up at the Browns' house.

Chapter Six

FOR SATURDAY EVENING, Vicky took extra care with her appearance, donning a vibrant red dress with little white polka dots. A dress she'd received from her girlfriends on her last birthday but hadn't worn yet. Berta and Evie would be pleased to see it. Vicky even put on nail polish she'd purchased that week for this evening's occasion.

Her preparations, and the added issue of some inevitable jitters, took up more time than she'd scheduled for herself. She arrived at the Browns' house nearly a half-hour later than she would have otherwise, fidgeting with the unbuttoned sweater resting over her shoulders.

When Willie opened the front door for her, his smile was huge. And relieved. "Hey! You made it. I was starting to worry."

As he'd promised, no pajamas were in sight tonight. Willie's casual shirt was topped with a sharp sport suit, and Vicky admired how the jacket set off the build of his shoulders. She smiled up at him, asking, "Oh, so your dad isn't the only Brown around who worries?"

Willie chuckled, leaning to his right to put up a wave, sending off Vicky's father who'd been watching out from his car. As Vicky stepped inside to the sound of music, Willie offered, "I'll put your stuff...your things down, if you want."

Handing her sweater and shoulder bag to him as he closed the door, she told him, "I'm sorry I'm late. I must be the last to get here."

"Well. Maybe that means you're the best." When Willie's meaning didn't hit her right away, he said, "You can't really 'save' the best for first."

"Oh. Right." Vicky gave a small laugh, turning to look further into the living room.

That's when the reverse of a gust happened, coming in the form of a gasp instead of a sigh from her.

Most of the furniture had been pushed to the edges of the room, with a table full of sandwiches, snacks, and a punch bowl visible in the adjoining dining room. Willie's guests as well as Vicky's additional invitees were indeed already present, and as a new record started up, the guests weren't merely listening to the swinging music in the place. With the exception of a few who were busy eating, and Bam, who was only bobbing his head as he stood by the open record player cabinet, all of the guests in the living room were dancing.

Vicky stood frozen. Staring. She should have guessed it beforehand. It was more than understandable that when a bunch of teenagers would get together on a Saturday night to listen to records, dancing would be a likely part of the activity. Especially when there was sufficient room for it, as there was in the Browns' house when the furniture was so situated.

Of course.

"Vicky?" Willie's lowered voice came to her, somewhat behind her but close to her side. "You okay?"

It wasn't a question she wanted him to feel he had to ask her. Not here at a party he'd invited her to.

Vicky continued studying the room, with more intention now. "I take it your dad's upstairs."

"Yup. Says he's bound to stop back down to steal more sandwiches whenever, though. Miss Mavis made so many of 'em before she went home."

Vicky didn't budge from her spot, finding she rather liked having Willie's voice, his presence, hovering close over her shoulder. "Bam is by himself," she pointed out.

Willie followed her line of vision. "No he isn't. He really likes music, but he can't dance. So when people are over here, he mans the record player and picks the songs. In between his trips to get grub."

"Bam can't dance?"

A grunt sounded from Willie. "He says no girl would want to be within a hundred feet of him if he tried."

Vicky's lips bunched to one side in thought. "But he's got rhythm."

As she and Willie watched more of Bam's head-bobbing, Willie said, "His big ol' dome does, anyway."

"Yeah. And does he like to clown around?"

"Clown around? Plenty."

Vicky bit one side of her bottom lip. No, she hadn't guessed about this when she probably should have. Hadn't prepared herself for the prospect of attending a weekend dance.

Even so, it was a private party without that big of a crowd. What was more, she was here now.

Taking a breath, she turned to Willie, saying, "Maybe you could man the record player for the next song. Put on something fun but kind of easy?"

The look that came over Willie's face reminded Vicky of someone who could get caught up in physically acting out a thrilling story to entertain his listener. So caught up that he might forget for a minute that a person of his self-proclaimed freight-truckish size should watch where he was going.

Willie couldn't be any stranger to clowning around himself.

"You're gonna dance with Bam?" he asked Vicky, a dash of impishness sprinkled over the question.

Vicky held a conspiratorial finger up to her lips. So, Willie took off toward the record player, setting Vicky's bag and sweater down beside a short row of others on the back of the displaced couch on the way.

As the current song reached its finish, Vicky wound a path through the guests on the informal dance floor. She patted a quick hello on Berta's shoulder but didn't draw her away from Howard. Vicky continued on to the dining room to get a hold of Evie, who stepped away from a chat she'd been a part of at the punch bowl.

"*Ooo*, lovebug," Evie greeted her. "You're wearing the dress! See? What'd we tell you? It's perfect on you. We were about to phone and check if you were still coming." She leaned in to whisper, "Willie was worrying."

Vicky's smile was a shy one. "Thank you, thank you, but no need for worries. I've got to borrow you for something."

"Borrow me?"

"Yes, please. Come on."

It didn't take Vicky long to work out the arrangement she had in mind. While Willie took over the record player, Vicky beckoned Bam away from it, leading Evie onto the dance floor.

Bam's eyes were large as Vicky spoke hushed instructions to him. When the sound of The King Cole Trio popped onto the record player with "Straighten Up and Fly Right," Vicky spun around to Evie with a command.

"Dance!"

Evie dithered with a baffled laugh, and Vicky motioned for her to get going. "Dance, doggone it!"

Accordingly, Evie began bopping to the music. As Vicky backed away, she signaled to Bam with her fingers. "Go 'head, Bam!"

With a shrug, he got to it, lowering himself a little and starting to throw down snaps of his fingers toward Evie's feet to the beat.

Vicky moved to the outskirts of the dance floor, smiling over at her handiwork. *Hm. It does almost look like they're both doing something. Go figure.*

It must not have mattered much that Vicky's instructions only got Bam partway through the song. He and Evie were soon laughing enough that when she took hold of his hands to simply bop his and her way through the rest of the number, Bam didn't seem to mind that she was clearly the one leading their dance.

Afterward, Willie seemed stuck somewhere between heading up a round of applause for his friend—"Aw, man, you bad!"—and heaving a long guffaw. He turned the honor of record player duty back over to Bam, who stopped to take a bow first. Evie was still laughing as she scampered over to

Vicky, who thought to do some applauding herself. But it struck her that Evie's laughter sounded watery, matching a damp shine that had come to her reddening eyes.

Vicky stepped closer to her friend, reaching down to take one of her hands. "Evie?"

Evie started to shake her head, but when her smile trembled, Vicky turned and led her to the kitchen. In the second or two that it took Vicky to make sure the kitchen was empty of others, Berta slipped into the room too, saying, "Saw you sneak out. Something the matter?"

Evie groaned, recovering her hand so that she could put both of hers up to her cheeks. "Oh, no. I'm sorry. I was going to come and just try to enjoy the night. Didn't want to ruin it for anybody else."

So far, it sounded like whatever had upset Evie, it was something other than straightening up and flying right with Bam. Still, Vicky was about to ask if her arrangement had been an awful idea after all when Evie blurted, "I'm leaving."

Berta's jaw dropped with concern. "You're leaving the party? Already?"

"No, no." Evie's hands fell from her face. "West Hill. Leaving Port Milestone. My parents said. Last night."

A sinking feeling crept into Vicky's stomach. "Leaving Port Milestone? Why?"

Evie shook her head. "Because of my great-grandma and everything since the summer. The family house was hers. She had a lot of strict rules about inheriting it. It turns out that my dad is the oldest living family member who didn't break any of her rules. When she brought her will up to date before she died, she said that my dad gets the house." Evie's damp eyes welled up further. "So we're moving into it. As soon as my parents can sell our house. I mean—the house we live in. They think it'll sell fast too. Lots of families looking to buy homes since the war."

Vicky and Berta only stood there for a moment.

Evie's great-grandmother's house. Almost halfway across the country.

Evie let out a glum rush of air. "It'll actually be a good move for my dad's work. The engineering. We'll be closer to some of my mom's relatives too. And they say there're some great schools around there." A drop from Evie's eye spilled over, her voice reducing to nothing but breath. "But it won't be like living in Black Diamond."

Perhaps Vicky's mental reaction was on account of whose house she was standing in. After she thought of her home right then, her next thought was of Bro Brown's Burgers and Malts.

"It's a good spot for the neighborhood. The people."

Vicky considered the sense of community for which Willie had, in his way, expressed having a deep appreciation. A deep connection. Though she could take it for granted at times, it was a connection Vicky shared.

She wasn't unaware that, in the forming of her career aspirations, she didn't have dreams of going off to work at a famous newspaper in one hustling metropolis or another, or a scenario as close to that as possible. Her natural thought and the draw within her was toward the newspaper published by West Hill.

"I bet I wouldn't even have to leave Black Diamond. I could work for the Courier.*"*

Then there were the parades and promenades down Main Street. Football and basketball games. Walks to the grocery, and a well-informed bag boy. Walks to the library, and a no-nonsense Miss Tatum. The jukebox available at a prime location, full of coins and a mix of song selections, including music refused by certain radio stations. Neighborhood streets where children were safe to run around doing a bunch of nothing, with real homes for them to run back to afterward.

All of it and more passed through Vicky's mind, through her heart, in a flash.

"Man! It's something, Vicky."

Yes. It was. And it was quite an aspect of it all when a girl, one who wouldn't call herself popular, happened to have a nickname at school, and the owner of the spot on Main for burgers and malts knew about the nickname. Even when it had been years since the childhood times when the girl used to visit that business owner's house.

Life in her community was comprised of so much, down to the everyday details. Here, now, with one of her best friends telling her she was leaving Black Diamond, Vicky couldn't take any of those details for granted.

Berta was the first to move forward, wrapping her arms around Evie. Vicky wasn't far behind, locking the three of them in a tight embrace.

Their trio was in no hurry to leave the kitchen.

Later on that evening, Vicky was sitting on the displaced couch in the living room, nibbling on an oatmeal cookie. Brother Brown had made a trip downstairs some time ago, picking up more sandwiches and disappearing again. Berta and Howard were among others on the dance floor but weren't exactly dancing, the two of them having nestled into a hug with minimal swaying. They didn't look out of place, as Bam had begun easing the music away from swinging and boogie-woogie tunes. If he, stationed in place on record player duty, hadn't been by himself before, he was even less so now, proving to be fitting company for a girl who wasn't feeling up to any more dancing. Evie was at Bam's side, and he'd settled a companionable arm over her shoulders.

Vicky, watching the two of them, had to swallow past a lump that wasn't a bite of cookie.

She was finishing up her snack when Willie left a conversation at the food table and walked back into the living room.

He came over to the couch, lowering himself to sit beside Vicky. "No, my dad isn't the only Brown who worries," he told her. When she gave him a questioning look, he added, "I can't tell if you're having a good time anymore."

He hadn't asked a question, technically, but it was an inquiry anyhow. Another one that Vicky didn't want him to feel he had to put out there. "This isn't my usual Saturday," she answered. "I would normally be curled up with a book right now." She brought up her fingers, flickering them like marquee lights around her face. "Shocking, I know." Willie gave a quiet laugh, and Vicky turned off the flashing lights, letting him know, "That doesn't mean I'm not glad you invited me here, though. Because I am."

"Really?"

"Really."

Willie only stared at her before he nodded. "Good. Because, uh..." He opened his hands, indicating more of the room. "I like everybody I invited, and yeah, this isn't the first time I've had people over or anything." His hands fell to his knees. "But the main reason I did today was so you would come."

After she went motionless for a second, Vicky's hand went up to her chest. "Me?"

"Yup. I was kicking myself after homecoming, so my dad said I should try this. That's when Miss Mavis said I should write to you about it." Willie's head angled this way and that with a hesitant confession. "I wanted to ask you to the homecoming dance. Well, I was going to ask if you wanted me to be your date, since, you know. I owe you."

Vicky let out an amused, mildly disputing breath but hadn't time to comment as Willie went on. "I was about to do it when I gave you the peanut butter and jelly, but that wasn't the best time. Then I started thinking later about how I didn't remember ever seeing you at a dance before. Then I heard you told Chester Cunningham 'not in a million years,' even with his chauffeur and everything." The smile that wavered over Willie's face had only so much humor in it. "So what chance did I have?"

Vicky couldn't reply right away, needing to confirm to herself that she was hearing him correctly. "You—you didn't ask me to homecoming because you thought I'd say no?"

The answer was in Willie's somewhat embarrassed expression, leaving no need for him to speak it. "But you've been over here plenty of times," he said instead. "Back in the day, anyway, and you came again the other week. So, I figured..." His hands gestured toward the room again.

Vicky's hand lowered from her chest as she inwardly completed his thought, letting it sink in. It was then time for her to bring clarity to a few particulars. "I didn't say anything about a million years to anybody. You know how rumors can be."

Willie yielded a nod of admission. "Oh. True."

"Yeah. Anyway, I'm not interested in Chester Cunningham. I don't think he's really interested in me either." Vicky paused, not quite decided on how much she wanted to disclose about all she'd imagined on this matter. Still, she was certain she wanted to be honest. "As for never seeing me at a dance—I've never gone to one because if, um... If I try to dance with somebody, I might stumble around. Or fall. In front of everybody."

Following that, she couldn't tell what was reflected in Willie's face. Confusion? A degree of understanding? Did he look fairly, well, charmed?

Maybe it was some blend of it all.

When Willie spoke up, his voice was basically a whisper. "Hey. Lemons and Honey Girl," he began, causing her very attention to lean nearer to him. "Do you think I'd let you fall?"

As a backdrop to that question, Ella Fitzgerald's audible presence happened to be gracing their gathering, singing "It's Only a Paper Moon." It wasn't an unfitting time for that song, since Vicky had to get a better grasp on how much, at this point, she believed in the guy sitting beside her. A guy who, on the one hand, she was getting to know, and on the other hand, she'd known for practically all her life.

In the space of a few heartbeats, she was back at the end of summer break. Back in the middle of Bro Brown's. Captured from cancelled toppling. Leaning in Willie's hold.

Sure, the trained reflexes of an athlete must have helped him to catch her so fast. But because he hadn't been fast in letting her go, she'd had that space in time to imagine dancing. To imagine being dipped. Time to blink up into the rich brown face of this boy from the neighborhood...who was no longer just a boy from the neighborhood.

Did she think he would let her fall?

Vicky blinked a couple of times now. Not on account of a daze in this instance but because of a mist in her eyes. An agreeable mist, to be sure, but she blinked to keep it under control. Her head moved from side to side, the movement faint but convinced, the retreating mist leaving the evidence of a warm, rising wish in its place.

Willie must have seen it rise. As his gaze searched hers, he observed, "Besides, Bam isn't playing music to stumble to, at the moment. Huh?"

Not a bad way to describe the more leisurely atmosphere that now permeated the party. Willie rose from the couch and turned to Vicky, extending a hand to her. Asking her. Risking whatever odds that she could still say no.

As if she would.

Vicky reached to accept Willie's hand, allowing him to draw her up from the couch and toward the others on the floor.

There was a break in the music, and then The King Cole Trio returned. The velvety voice of Nat "King" Cole was liquid chocolate, slowly pouring into the room with "(I Love You) For

Sentimental Reasons" as Willie began leading Vicky into...a dance.

Gentle. Close, but not confining.

Vicky had dreamed of going on library dates. She'd dreamed of connecting with a guy over books. Over the compelling use of language as communication. Yet, this gentle, close experience wrapped in melody—this, too, was the mutual sharing of language. Not only as a matter of the song's loving lyrics. Perhaps not even mainly in the lyrics, but the music itself was also a language.

And this, this was a language as well: the lingering look between Willie's eyes and Vicky's. Something for which she didn't have any English just now, which didn't matter.

Willie's hand curled in around hers, his arm around her back taking the chance to ease her closer. She, holding on to his shoulder, took the chance to lay her head against it. *Mm. Wow.* Somehow, in the midst of all the anxious notions she'd had about stumbling and falling in the heat of jazzy action, she'd failed to consider how smooth and soothing this style of music could be sometimes.

The rumble of a tender chuckle in Willie's throat made her aware of how near she'd brought her face to his neck. Was that only a chuckle of general pleasure from him, or had her hair or something tickled him? She'd have to stop by a mirror after this to check on her hair. Wouldn't want resting against Willie this way to leave her looking a mess.

Another low hum from him assured her that it wasn't a mere surface reaction, as though from being tickled. He brushed his jaw against her forehead, and her heart stirred. So did her curiosity.

Hmm. If Willie with the Beard chose to go against the grain someday and, of all things, to actually grow a beard—would it scratch?

The question in Vicky's head brought a laugh to her chest, and she let it settle there.

When the song ended, Vicky's feet paused from moving with Willie's, but she showed no intention of leaving his arms, and he didn't take them away from her. Within seconds, the same song started right over again.

Whatever Bam's purpose was in making that choice, Vicky sent a silent blessing his way. Willie continued to lead her small steps with his through smooth melody, velvety chocolate, and awakening possibilities of sentimental reasons.

Vicky's eyes slipped to a close. No, this wasn't her normal Saturday evening. She didn't receive invitations like this every day, but once she had received this one, she'd had no doubt about where she wanted to be tonight.

She'd been right.

IN THE AFTERGLOW OF Willie's party, Vicky had no trouble tapping into inspiration for her next Life Beat article.

Food!

What she was getting together wasn't exactly a recipe, in her opinion, but it would do. On Monday after school, her mother found her at the kitchen counter at home with slices from a loaf of bread and jars of peanut butter, grape jelly, and strawberry jam.

"For Life Beat," Vicky explained. "Trying to decide if I like the grape or the strawberry better with peanut butter." After some further munching, she decided mostly to herself, "I'll tell the kids to experiment with different ones," then she said to her mother, "I hear that our troops ate these at war."

Her mother nodded, coming over to cut a corner of the grape version on the counter for herself. "It's true. While I was still serving food at the canteen after the end, some soldiers coming back from overseas would mention what they ate while they were over there. Peanut butter and jelly included."

"Oh?" Vicky's eyebrows popped up. "Mom, may I quote you in the article?" She nodded down at her notepad and pencil sitting near the loaf of bread.

Her mother bit into the sandwich corner she'd snagged. "Hm! Victoria Phillips, my dear columnist. Will that make me one of your *sources*, honest to goodness?"

Vicky laughed, taking another bite of sandwich for herself.

Her article wasn't submitted ahead of schedule like her first, but it was a fun one to write. She included tips such as: "Be sure to use enough spread on both slices so that the bread won't soak it all up before you eat it."

She did indeed incorporate what she'd heard about wartime troops from Marion Phillips, a former volunteer at the railroad canteen outside of Port Milestone that provided free food to the nation's soldiers during the war.

To top it off, Vicky encouraged a sense of patriotism in her recommendation of this "all-American source of protein, sweetness, and satisfaction."

There was a key factor that she left out of the column, however. While she found the sandwiches she made to be quite tasty, they weren't the ambrosia on bread she'd melted over the very first time.

The literal ingredients of a dish or a snack—or a gift—must not have been all that would determine its taste.

Chapter Seven

UNLIKE HER PEANUT BUTTER and jelly article, there was a different piece of writing that Vicky finished ahead of schedule. As part of a joint effort.

She and Thomas finished co-writing their narrative poem for English class the week before it was due. While they were sitting at a table in the school library after classes one afternoon, they agreed that their piece was complete.

"This is great," Thomas said with a grin, neatening their few papers together on the table. "I couldn't have done it without you."

"You weren't supposed to do it without me," Vicky pointed out with a chortle. "Unless you were trying to be a free ride to an A plus."

Thomas laughed, clearly trying to keep his voice down as he did so. "No, I mean the choice to go with rhyming instead of free verse. If I'd tried to make a whole poem rhyme by myself, it would've sounded corny." He slid the papers closer to his co-writer, his expression softening. "But you made it beautiful."

Vicky's thoughts hiccupped over that unexpected praise. She inwardly scrambled for a way to pass the weight of it back over to Thomas. "And you're the one who made it a story." She picked up a pencil to shake at him. "I bet if you wanted to write the next *Paradise Lost* or something, you could."

"I would need you. To help me with timing the stanzas. We work well together, Vicky." Thomas hesitated, drumming the fingers of one hand on the table before he said, "Maybe now we should try playing together."

Vicky almost dropped her pencil. "What?"

A breath of laughter rode over a nervous bump in Thomas's voice. He shifted sideways in his seat, resting his forearm on the table, leaning toward Vicky. "Would you like to go see a movie with me sometime?"

Both of Vicky's hands gripped the pencil, turning it back and forth like a key stuck in a lock. "As a date?"

"Yes. As a date." Another bumpy laugh escaped Thomas. "Since you seem to think going to the library together doesn't count."

"Hm? That's different. We *had* to study with a partner for this assignment."

"Well, would you like to be my partner at a movie? Maybe this weekend?"

With the key showing no sign of getting the lock to release, Vicky slowly set her pencil down on the table. "Um, I've heard it can get complicated when colleagues decide to date." An amused tilt came to Thomas's head, and Vicky said, "We should stay focused on getting our poem turned in, see what grade we get."

Thomas spread his hands before him with confidence. "I already know we get an A."

"Still." Vicky veered course, patting a palm on their papers. "Even though it isn't required for the assignment, I can type this up for us. In the newsroom."

"No, no. I can do that. I have a typewriter at home." Thomas took the papers back, sliding them into a folder. "When you're in the newsroom, all you should worry about is working your journalistic magic."

A tiny thrill sparkled its way through Vicky, a surprised smile touching her face. "My magic?"

"Yes. You've got some. Like a little fairy." It was possible that the flittering of Thomas's fingers was meant to resemble the sprinkling of fairy dust. "I absolutely *ate up* your peanut butter and jelly sandwich article," he remarked with a chuckle. "It was cute."

More praise? This time, it didn't strike Vicky like a weight to pass off but rather like a minor chord with a wayward note caught somewhere in the middle. She sat up straighter, her memory skimming over that last piece she'd written for the newspaper. "A tad sentimental, maybe," she allowed with a murmur, on account of the private reasons that had inspired her to write on that particular topic. She then raised her voice to its previous notch to say, "But I meant it to be patriotic too."

"Oh, it was. It was," Thomas agreed. "In a cute way."

Vicky's psyche might not have bristled at that, exactly. It did prickle, however. "Well." She searched around for another allowance. "I do still need more journalistic practice." As she offered that statement to the both of them, it effectively added wood chips to the small flame of misgiving she already had about the prospect of her next article.

The day before, Hester had stopped Vicky in a school hallway to tell her, "Nice job you've been doing on the lifestyle and society column so far. But it could use more on the 'society' side. We'll talk after the next *Daily* meeting." The smile that had fanned over Hester's face could have been a floral folding fan snapping open. Partially. "I have a scoop for you."

Any columnist or other reporter should have been pleased to hear that. Right? Nonetheless, the resulting flame that ignited for Vicky wasn't one that got her too excited about whatever Hester had in store for her.

In any case, Vicky's train of thought steered onto a more promising track with a question that followed from Thomas. "Do you plan on studying journalism in college?"

Vicky's hearing perked up. Although she hadn't let Thomas know she was specifically planning on college, she didn't at all mind that he'd made the assumption. "Yes. Yes, I do."

"That's good," he voiced his approval with a nod. "It'll give you something to do while you're there."

The alert condition of Vicky's hearing lost its perk aspect. Her eyebrows inched closer together, likely prompting Thomas to go on to explain, "You won't be one of those girls who only go there to skip around campus, trying to land a college man."

The promising track for her train of thought was looking more like a promise fated to go unfulfilled. Vicky's next words were unrushed. Deliberate. "No. I'm going to study journalism in college so that I can be a journalist."

After a few more nods apparently riding on the back of Thomas's previous word of approval, his head halted. "Wait." Lines appeared along his brow. "As a job, you mean?"

"As a career. Yes."

A second passed, and then Thomas brushed his hand to the side. "Oh, you won't need a job, Vicky. You're not a girl who'll have trouble getting a husband."

"Excuse me?" The question shot out of Vicky's mouth at a higher volume than she'd intended. She reined herself in but didn't leave Thomas time to repeat or rephrase his comment before she went on, holding up a finger before her as she asked, "Why would I go to college for journalism if I didn't want to be a journalist?"

"Why would you?" Thomas appeared puzzled. "Why wouldn't you? Every girl who wants to go to college should go. Especially if she's serious about gaining more knowledge. Serious about her studies. It'll give her one more major academic experience before she settles down in real life."

Vicky's finger stayed put in the air. As if standing frozen in time.

Thomas smiled at her. "I could see you being good at it. Your real life. Being a wife, I mean. You've got sense. A good reputation, from what I've heard. You're easy to get along with." A pinkish tinge rose behind the freckles on his golden brown cheeks as he added, "You're pretty."

His mild blush took Vicky aback. A moment went by before she found her voice again. "Thank you." She finally lowered her finger, but her straightened posture in her seat remained as it was. "I can be all that and a good journalist too."

Thomas studied her as if trying to gauge the level of authenticity behind her declaration. His head tipped at a patient angle as he gave her a steady look, his voice dropping. "No real man wants his wife working. If he's doing his job, she doesn't need to." It was plain that a new thought hit him then, his head coming upright. "That is...you do want to be married, don't you?"

Vicky's look was just as steady. Unblinking. Her chin dipped a degree, her voice also dropping.

Dropping a question on the floor of their conversation with a pronounced thud. "To you?" she asked Thomas.

He went still. Stiff. He was gauging again.

For the most part, he'd maintained his lean toward Vicky since he'd made his inquiry about this coming weekend. Now, Thomas sat up.

"Well." He cleared his throat, reaching for the folder on the table. "So, um, I'll get this all typed up tonight. Or tomorrow."

Vicky's thoughts regrouped somewhat. She held up a hand. "You don't have to. Other homework to do, and all that."

"I want to." Setting the folder on top of his schoolbooks, Thomas gave Vicky a half-smile. "You had a good idea about typing it. We wrote a great poem. Might as well make it look our best."

"Oh. All right." Vicky turned and began gathering her belongings on the table, packing her book bag.

When she rose out of her seat, Thomas hurried to do the same, saying, "Gosh, Vicky. Was this a fight? It kind of feels like a fight. I don't want us to do that."

Vicky stared at him, pulling the strap of her book bag over her shoulder.

Thomas's mouth slanted. "Does this mean you don't want to go to a movie?"

It was Vicky's turn to do some gauging, as her initial notion told her that Thomas must be putting a joke out there to lighten the air between them. When she didn't detect any humor in his gaze, she indicated the folder in front of him with one hand. "Let's just get that A on our poem. All right?"

Thomas wavered on his feet, and then he gave a conceding nod, his knuckles tapping down on the folder. "Right."

After he and Vicky said their goodbyes, she was quick in making her departure from the school library. It wasn't only on account of the sudden stinging behind her eyes, threatening to dampen them. It had more to do with her own perplexity, as she couldn't tell what strong emotion within her must have brought on the stinging.

Then, as much as Vicky didn't want to admit it to herself, Thomas's remarks about her "cute" article writing were in the back of her mind during the school newspaper meeting later that week.

Some of the staff filed out of the newsroom afterward, with a couple of them staying behind to sit down at a typewriter or to finish flying a new set of scratch paper darts. Hester held up a staying finger toward Vicky before disappearing from the room, so Vicky moseyed over to one of the windows. She stood looking out, tapping the top of a pencil on the waiting notepad in her hand.

A few minutes later, Hester reentered through the newsroom door, striding in on the arm of a student who wasn't one of the school paper's staff members.

Chester Cunningham.

He and Hester came and stood before Vicky, Hester announcing, "I'm sure the student body will be happy to read in your column that Chester and Hester are back together."

Vicky tried to ignore the extra noisy shuffling of papers that happened to start up over at the editor's desk. Ed must have been far too busy to have heard the announcement. Or to do any subsequent listening.

The fact that Hester had done the announcing gave Vicky an excuse not to focus on whatever kind of smile was plastered on Chester's face. She mostly directed her congratulations at Hester and asked, "What other details would you like to share?"

In the minutes that followed, Hester did all of the sharing, hanging on to Chester's arm the entire time. What with the way the romantic couple and the society columnist seemed to have made an unspoken agreement to remain standing for this interview, Vicky had to tamp down the temptation to interrupt the proceedings and to bellow out, "Dearly beloved, we are gathered here today..."

After the interview, Hester sent Chester off on his way. Once he'd left the newsroom, Hester turned back to Vicky, saying, "Off the record. I'm not sure how much you heard about our misunderstanding over the summer. Mine and Chester's. But it made him think he needed to prove that he's not shallow. So, he figured he'd prove it by dating a..." She indicated Vicky with rolling flaps of her hand, searching for the right label.

Vicky's brows rose. More accurately, it was only one of her brows, arching to encourage—or to challenge—Hester along in her search.

Hester halted her flapping, dropping her hand. "I..." She gave her head a shake and held it high, pulling back her shoulders. "Whatever Chester said to you. Around homecoming or whenever. It wasn't personal."

Vicky's eyebrow held its position a bit longer. "I never thought it was."

Hester started to reply but stopped, her eyes blinking wider, her mouth wandering between closing and opening.

Taking a step forward, Vicky moved her pencil and pad to the same hand. She held her free hand out to Hester and said, "All right?"

After a moment of further blinking and a short, airy titter, Hester relaxed her shoulders. She reached to accept the handshake, giving Vicky a small smile. "All right."

Hester was the next to leave the newsroom. Vicky watched her go and then glanced over at Ed, who happened to be looking her way. He grinned, giving Vicky a thumbs-up.

While she responded to the gesture with an attempt at a smile, she couldn't help the sigh that rose up and streamed out of her.

AT HOME ON AN EVENING during the following week, Vicky was lounging in bed in her pajamas, reading a novel by the light of the lamp on her nightstand. She was in the middle of a chapter when a soft knock sounded on her bedroom door, preceded by her mother's voice.

After Vicky bid her to enter, her mother stepped inside, wearing a bathrobe over a nightgown, her hair not yet rolled and wrapped up for the night. She closed the door behind her. "I wanted to catch you before you fell asleep. You were pretty quiet at dinner." She came and sat down near the end of Vicky's bed. "Feeling down about Evie?"

"Oh. A little." Vicky slid her novel aside. "But I guess I was thinking about my next article for the school paper. I submitted it today."

"Ah. I see. Are you not happy about that for some reason?"

Vicky adjusted one of her pillows in front of her headboard and sat up against it. Stalling. Sighing. Then doing her best to relay the last conversation she'd had with Thomas. Once she'd gotten through the words they'd exchanged, she said, "I don't really understand. It seemed like he appreciated my writing for our homework, but his compliment about my column felt..."

Her mother had pressed her lips together while listening. She now parted them to lend a suggestion to her daughter's unfinished thought. "Patronizing?"

"Um, yes. Patronizing." Vicky reached up with one hand to give herself a couple of pats on the head. Only light pats, on account of the rollers she'd put in her hair, covered with a headscarf. She deepened her voice. "Nice thing you're doing for the school newspaper, you little fairy. Keep up your magical little hobby until you settle down instead of working." Reverting back to her normal voice, she asked, "Do you think he was only complimenting my writing at first so I'd go to the movies with him?"

Vicky's mother tipped her head toward one lifting shoulder. "I couldn't say for sure. You're better acquainted with

Thomas than I am. But it seems to me, if his motive was just to sweet-talk you into a date, he'd probably be saying that everything you write is beautiful to him. Not only your way with poetry."

"Hm." Vicky had to think about that before she said, "Well, something about his attitude still rubbed me the wrong way." After pretending to give her head another pat, she let her hand fall. "He didn't have to be, you know, patronizing about it, but he maybe did have a point. About my column, anyway." She shook her head. "I can tell for myself that something is missing. So far."

Her mother gave her an even look. "What do you mean?"

"I mean that Life Beat isn't really the kind of writing I want to do. Or not what I want my writing to be? I'm not sure how to say it, but something is missing." Vicky brought her knees up, putting her arms around them over her covers. "I know the real reason I enjoyed writing about peanut butter and jelly in the first place is because of Willie."

"Willie?"

"Yeah, Willie-with-the... Willie Brown made me a sandwich. Brought it to me at school."

Vicky's mother leaned over onto her side at the end of the bed, propping herself up on her elbow. "Did he now?"

"He sure did. It was sweet of him. Then his party was so nice, and I was feeling so good afterwards, I picked peanut butter and jelly as a Life Beat topic. My first article was actually because of Willie too, but it was only my second best idea for that, I think. I would have wanted to do an interview with Willie for Homecoming Week, but that would've been stepping on Donald's territory. He does sports for the paper."

A snort got away from Vicky. "Goofs around and doesn't turn in his articles until right before press time, though. One of these days, he might wind up getting stuck in the machine at the printer's because he's trying to hurry up and write something on the paper before it pops out the other end."

Vicky's mother laughed but didn't say anything as her daughter continued. "Then today, I submitted an article about Chester and Hester being boyfriend and girlfriend again. That's good for them, and yes, the student body does love reading about who's dating. But is that news *I* want to be writing about? No. And if it hadn't been for Willie and how I was, um, how I'm...feeling about him, I would've felt silly picking sandwiches as a news topic."

Vicky briefly flipped up one hand from its hold around her knees. "Not that there's anything wrong with writing about food. Editor Ed mentioned about how recipes and fashion are relevant, and he's right. But I don't like the idea that the reason I got assigned to Life Beat is because I'm a girl. Ed was clear that that's why. And I bet Thomas would agree with that choice. As if recipes and clothes and romance are the only things that a little fairy should write about for a newspaper."

She came to a pause, the fingers of one hand picking pensively at the covers over her legs. "It's funny, when I think about it. It seems like before—maybe even earlier this year—I would've been so excited about meeting a boy like Thomas. He's such a good student and not a bad guy." One corner of Vicky's mouth inched upward. "Before, I probably would have saved some of his carnations. Would've pressed them into a book or something. Instead of throwing them away when they dried out."

Her mother remained resting on her elbow, waiting, and then she spoke up. "You know, as we grow and gain some experience, it's normal for some of our desires to change. Not everything in life will fit exactly into the first ideas we had. But that's part of the beauty of living. Finding out more than we imagined at first."

A wrinkle came to Vicky's forehead. When she didn't reply, her mother smiled, sitting up. "People can surprise you, Victoria. Your father, for one, surprised me. All of that...that personality *busting* out of him when I met him. Ah!" Her head bobbled with a girlish laugh. "But Lord knows I needed that man. He's been well worth finding out about, and that's the truth."

She reached out a hand, patting it down beside Vicky's covered feet. "Pay attention to what's happening inside you, deep down. Pay attention to your God-given conscience. And don't be afraid whenever you find out more. More than what you first thought about this or that."

Vicky sat there making the effort to wrap her mind around that word of counsel. She'd need more time to mull over it.

Her mother sat back, saying, "As for journalism being, what, a nice hobby for you until you settle down instead of working?" She tossed a hand in the air. "Women have always been working. Always. The world is full of our work—and yes, homemaking is a big part of that. Nobody can tell me I don't work hard day after day, making this home what it is."

Her eyes turned reflective, with more gravity than reverie. "Then the war proved another aspect of our mettle. Many more women than usual went marching into the labor force. Housewives too. It showed more people that the home isn't the only place of work—isn't the only *kind* of work—where women are capable." Her gaze had a firm hold on Vicky's now. "And I hear you, you know. I'm listening. Including when you talk about Ida B. Wells. She's such an inspiration, and you've got to remember that she's one among other women whose work..."

Vicky's mother's fingers lifted, holding an invisible pen, making the motion of writing into space and time as she completed her point. "Whose *work* we all needed. All of us. Even people in this country who don't know it."

A certain sensation, then, wasn't the same. It wasn't the same as it had been the week before, when Vicky had made her quick, perplexed departure from the school library.

The stinging that started behind her eyes was different tonight. And this time, the likelihood that her eyes would indeed dampen didn't strike her as a threat.

Vicky's mother's hand settled not beside but right atop her daughter's feet this time. "You were born who you are, with your gifts that are growing, for a reason. If you believe that your writing should be more than what it is right now, you should look further into that."

When Vicky's vision blurred, she blinked to clear it but not to hinder the warm drop that swelled through and slipped over her eyelid. The damp bead trickled as a salve, acknowledged by her mother's affirming smile. A smile paired with one more affirming thought. "You wouldn't be feeling so strongly about it if it were nothing."

Chapter Eight

THE NEXT MORNING AS Vicky sat in the kitchen eating her breakfast, she was again rather quiet. She had a feeling, though, that her mother wasn't too worried about it in this case.

Roy had already left the house to get down to the shipyard, and Vicky's father was getting ready to head out to the bank. Her mother got up from the breakfast table to follow him into the living room and to send him off with the end of their chat. Vicky looked over at the two of them in the other room while her father put on his coat, but he didn't put on his hat when he grabbed it. Instead, he interrupted whatever his wife was saying by holding the hat above her and letting it fall to perch on her head.

Plop.

She hadn't done her hair yet this morning. Consequently, the hat landed at a lopsided angle over her headscarf with rollers lumping up underneath it.

"Otis!" she squeaked.

In response to her husband's snickering, she took his hat off and held it out of his reach behind her back.

Well. Not quite out of his reach.

"Marion..."

To avoid witnessing whatever lovey-dovey means her father would no doubt be using to reclaim possession of his hat from his wife, Vicky turned back to her breakfast. Practically buried her face in her plate.

It was at that moment when memory began taking the opportunity to revisit her. In singular fashion.

Once her father was outside, making his way to his car parked in the drive, Vicky stood up to watch him from one of the kitchen windows.

"They thought our people weren't smart or able enough..."

As Vicky's father was opening his car door, he caught sight of his daughter in the kitchen window and paused, lifting his eyebrows. Did she want anything?

"That's why we have to make sure stuff gets written down. Keep records of who we are."

Vicky, in a bit of a haze, smiled and shook her head, giving her father a wave. He smiled in return, tipping his hat to her before he climbed into his car.

"...make sure stuff gets written down. Keep records of who we are. So people will know and remember."

His car backed out of the drive, turning, and Vicky watched as it disappeared down her neighborhood street.

Yet, more than the street held Vicky's gaze as she stood there for a while, lost—but not exactly lost—in the initial stirrings of an approaching idea.

"So people will know and remember."

Vicky's hand reached up to absently smooth her hair above her temple, a slight, pondering squint coming to her eyes.

Aside from the talkative lunch hour she spent with Berta and Evie later on, Vicky's attitude remained on the contemplative side for much of that school day.

Contemplating the homes dotting her neighborhood streets, one of which a best friend of hers was sad about leaving soon.

Thinking again about the Black Diamond Days parade that came each summer. The Christmas Promenade that came each winter. The special procession that came down Main after the war's end, in honor of war veterans who weren't so honored everywhere in the country.

Sporting events at West Hill Memorial Field.

Walks to the grocery. Walks to the library.

The jukebox. Standing in its prime location. Full of the community's coins. Kept supplied with a mix of America's music.

"It's a good spot for the neighborhood... It's something, Vicky."

By the time she'd reached the evening that day, after dinner, Vicky's stirring idea was no longer only approaching. It had arrived. Likely hastened by momentum that had begun well before this juncture.

Even so, Vicky had to take a breath to help calm a bundle of nerves as, before it got too late, she went to the living room and made a telephone call. Made a petitioning inquiry over the line. Expressed her earnest thanks as she set a weekend appointment.

Hence, at the end of that week, Saturday afternoon found Vicky seated at a table in Bro Brown's Burgers and Malts after the height of lunch hour, the jukebox thrumming for the light crowd that was present. Of course, it wasn't unusual for Vicky to be here at such a time, but today, it wasn't Berta and Evie who were seated with her.

Across the table from Vicky sat Brother Brown himself. In response to her telephone call, he'd said he would take a long lunch this afternoon, stating that his second cook "Ernie can handle the kitchen back there" while the owner of this establishment came out and had "a sit-down with Miss Vicky."

Some minutes earlier, before the purpose of this sit-down had gotten underway, the sight of Willie stepping out of the back, probably from the washroom, had caught Vicky's attention. He'd stopped walking when he saw her seated at a table with his father. Because Vicky didn't yet have a reporter hat with one of those little papers sticking up out of it, she held up her notepad and pencil for Willie to see.

After a second, he gave her a smile with equal measures of understanding and curiosity in it before he waved and headed out of the place. Then Vicky and Brother Brown got started.

The following week, when Vicky was again the first one to turn in her article for the school newspaper, Ed read her piece right away, as was his habit.

Alternating between reading in silence and reading in a mumble, he started fast but shifted to a thoughtful pace as he went along.

"...he wishes he could trace the Brown family tree further back than that. Yet, as it is in so many other Black families, his ancestors' identities in this country have been lost to history..."

"...had become a successful business owner, looking forward to the future for his growing family. Shortly after,

Brother Brown lost his wife and his unborn second son to childbirth..."

Finally, Ed raised his voice to his usual speaking level when he reached the last paragraph:

"So, the next time you and your friends stop by Brother Brown's brainchild for an afterschool soda, or you pop a coin in the jukebox before strolling up to order that juicy Saturday burger with a side of hot potato fries: eat, drink, and let those good times roll with gratitude. That neighborhood spot is a part of our community's soul, and our soul is what our people have never lost."

After the closing sentence, Ed fell quiet.

Vicky sat watching him from across his desk, the corner of her bottom lip rolling in and out of her mouth as she waited.

Leaning back in his seat, Ed reached up to take hold of the pencil he'd had tucked behind his ear. He began working the pencil through both sets of his fingers as he looked at Vicky, saying, "This...is different. More serious than the regular Life Beat."

Vicky nodded her admission to that. "Still a part of the overall lifestyle and society around here, though."

Ed's head moved slowly up and down. He sat up, skimming back over the article. "It's interesting how much his wife put into getting his idea off the ground."

Vicky agreed. "But she didn't want it to be called 'Brother and Sister Brown's Burgers'..."

"So strangers wouldn't think she was his sister..."

"And so it wouldn't sound too much to some people like the place must only be for church folks. Yeah." Vicky smiled a little at that.

Ed skimmed some more, and then he looked back up at Vicky. "You planning on any more articles like this?"

She took a moment before answering. "One of these days, I think I'll ask to interview the pastor and his wife at First Baptist. A lot of students either go there or have been to one of their community events." Vicky's smile grew. "Or have at least bought a plate of their chicken."

"*Whew*. Yes! That First Baptist *chicken*." Ed's eyes narrowed with recalled gratification. His fingers held his pencil in front of his mouth like a fried chicken thigh as he pretended to chew. Talking with his mouth full. "Make you wanna fool around and bust a leg off your own pants."

Vicky broke into a laugh. Despite being a girl who didn't wear pants too often, she shared her editor's First Baptist chicken sentiments precisely. Calming down, she added, "A lot of history comes with the first church in an area too. Pastor probably knows a lot of that stuff."

She held off to be sure Ed had finished his chicken and had sobered again, and she went on to say, "I'm writing Life Beat in *The Black Diamond Daily*, right? So I think it makes sense to start including more of the life of Black Diamond in it. The history." Her hand took up an invisible pen, briefly writing into space and time. "A part of keeping and sharing records about who we are."

As she set the pen down, she acknowledged, "I won't have something like this for every edition of the paper. But I think it'll be good to keep writing them occasionally. When I can come up with them."

Ed sat there thinking and then gave his pencil a sound tap on the piece she'd submitted. "Say, tell you what. You keep up with the regular Life Beat articles, and whenever you've got a different one like this, we'll call it a Life Beat Special that week. How's that?"

Vicky's heart of hearts stirred with a flip: tiny but pronounced. *A Life Beat Special.* A hopeful, pleased smile tugged on her lips. "That sounds good, Ed." She chuckled, correcting herself. "Editor Ed."

"Good." Rising to his feet as Vicky did, Ed held up her article. "This is solid, Phillips."

That word of praise didn't strike her as a weight to pass off or like a pat on the head or even a pat on her back. It brought more of an inward push to her, subtle but there.

A subtle and serious push forward. A challenge she'd come ready to accept.

The next week, Vicky awakened and rose early on the day her byline was due to appear on her first Life Beat Special in the *Daily*. As she washed and dressed for school, she hummed to herself, the tune of "Let the Good Times Roll" rolling from her hushed voice. It could have seemed like a frivolous song to accompany everything she was feeling this morning. But good times, good days, positive steps toward honest goals—they were all worth valuing. Worth celebrating.

She stood before her dresser mirror in her bedroom, reaching up to smooth her hair above her temples, staring at the two ample swirls pinned up on either side of her head. For now, it didn't matter that, fashion-wise, these particular feminine rolls of hair weren't as in style as they used to be, if they still were at all.

At the sight of her reflection, a smile came to Vicky's eyes. She wasn't ashamed about wearing this hairdo styled with care and intention, topping off her appearance as a curled crown.

It was a visual of victory.

IT WOULD TAKE SOME time for feedback from more than Vicky's editor and her friends to reach her in regard to her article. All the same, seeing her Special in print made for as encouraging a day for her as she'd expected it would. It gave her strength for the coming Saturday, when she and Berta spent the morning over at Evie's house.

As Evie's parents had predicted, it hadn't taken long for their house to sell. Their family was now in the process of packing. They wouldn't be taking everything with them, due to packing and traveling logistics and also because the house they were moving into was well-furnished.

Before Evie's departure, there were certain belongings of hers that she wanted to pass into the care of her two best friends. She'd told them to bring along some means of transporting a few items back home with them.

Vicky took her empty canvas bag along with her. Berta, on the other hand, showed up at Evie's house pulling a red toy wagon behind her.

"Uh, Bebe's wagon," Berta explained, referring to one of her younger sisters and leaving the wagon on the porch as Evie welcomed them into the house.

"If you say so," Vicky replied to Berta with a snicker. The two of them removed their coats, hanging them on the coat rack by the door before following Evie to her bedroom.

As they entered the bedroom, Evie told Berta, "It's actually fitting that you brought a toy for your transport purposes." Evie went and kneeled beside one of the open boxes on her bedroom floor. "Because I want you to take some of my stuffies. The ones I put in here," she said, reaching in to pull a stuffed animal out of the box, looking up at Berta. "You're the only other person our age who fully understands that stuffies are people."

"Aw, Evie." Berta scuttled over and got down on the floor to go digging into the box.

Evie left the animals to her and stood up, stepping over to the bed. "And I want you to take some of my books," she told Vicky, pointing out the two short stacks of books on the bed. "The ones you've borrowed before that I know you only gave back because you'd feel too guilty if you stole them."

Vicky laughed, walking over to the bed but shaking her head. "My goodness. Are you sure? Books are such a precious thing to let go of."

"The fact that you feel that way is why I'm entrusting them to you." Evie's smile wasn't entirely a happy one. "It'll save me a little needed packing space. And I can always get more books once I'm over there."

Vicky exhaled a wistful breath. *Way over there.* She smiled back at her friend. "We're going to miss you, you know."

Evie gave a husky chortle. "Oh, y'all won't have as much time to miss me as you think. You'll be too busy with your boyfriends."

Berta, with a stuffed toy in each hand, harrumphed with humor, but Vicky, darting her eyes between her friends, shook her head some more. Halfheartedly. "I don't have a boyfriend," she all but whispered.

"Oh, come on, Vick," Berta spoke up, jiggling the toys she held. "Everybody saw it."

The partial familiarity of that claim made Vicky's ears buzz. She didn't have to ask, "Saw what?" But she asked anyway.

"At the game last night," Evie said. "When Willie-with-the-Beard pointed the football at you again after a touchdown." She flapped a hand between herself and Berta. "We're not the only ones who can tell anymore. Now *everybody* knows he's pointing at you when he does that."

Vicky tried to still the excited fluttering of wings that started up in her middle. She failed miserably in doing so. "How do you know everybody knows? Did everybody come up to you and tell you they know?"

Berta jiggled her two toys toward each other. "Everybody doesn't have to tell us they know when we can tell they know. The football games are nice and public, with everybody looking. And people going '*ahh*' or gasping in the stands when Willie-with-the-Beard points up to the same girl at more than one game."

Tapping her pair of jiggling animals' mouths together, Berta made an exaggerated smooching noise before she said, "And this time, he did it after you wrote that super article about Bro Brown's and their family and everything? And after you wound up dancing the night away with Willie at his party? Oh, yeah. There's no way he's not your boyfriend. Or not going to be."

Vicky's failing fluttering management left her with little energy to do more than push out a teetering titter at that.

"Ah, the party," Evie sighed out on a high, dreamy note. "Bet you I would've left there with a boyfriend myself if I wasn't moving away. Bam was so cool about letting me stand there and be sad on his shoulder for most of the night. Other guys I've dated would've told me I was being a wet blanket. Or they would've tried to just flirt me out of my feelings."

The dropping of Berta's animals back into the box mirrored the drop in Vicky's heart. "Oh, Evie," she and Berta said at the same time.

Evie gave a resigned shrug, then she folded her arms, her tone shifting. "Speaking of my move, my lovebugs. Guess what I found out about the people who are buying this house? Or what I think I found out, anyway?"

"What?" Berta was swift to ask.

Evie peered from one of her friends to the other, apparently giving Vicky a chance to still put in a guess. When she didn't, Evie gave her answer, her voice carrying a degree of disbelief at her own declaration. "The people—the family moving in here. They're Mexican. As far as I know."

Vicky went motionless. Berta might have done the same before the two of them looked at each other. Both of their mouths opened, and nothing came out of either of them.

Vicky could almost feel a brand new type of wrinkle forming in one corner of her brain. *Oh, wow.*

A Mexican family. Moving to Black Diamond...

WHEN VICKY ARRIVED back at home that afternoon, she didn't make it to her bedroom. Roy wasn't home, and her parents were each occupied at some other corners of the house, leaving the living room empty.

That left Vicky immediate space to dig out the precious contents of her canvas bag and to spend some emotional time getting reacquainted with these gifts she already cherished.

She was sitting on the couch with an open book in her lap and more spread on the floor near her feet when the doorbell rang. It took her a minute to collect herself, to make fairly certain she wouldn't look too caught up in her emotions when she answered the door for whatever unannounced visitor was on the other side.

When she did go and open the front door, she was both surprised and delighted to find Willie on the front stoop, standing there in a pair of jeans and with his hands buried in the pockets of his letterman jacket. He appeared nervous but also glad and relieved to see her.

"Hey, Vicky. Gee, good thing it's you. I had a speech ready in case your mom or dad answered the door, but I forgot it that fast." Willie's smile wobbled. "Sorry I didn't call first. I could've been the one to catch you in your pj's this time. By accident."

Vicky smiled and gave her head a shake, speaking a quiet greeting to him. Wishing she could get her recurrence of inner fluttering under control.

Willie shifted his stance from one foot to the other. "Am I interrupting your homework? Or your writing or anything?"

Vicky took a step back from the door. "Oh, no, no. I was just reading. Sort of." She made a vague gesture in the general direction of the couch. "Um, would you like to come in?"

One of Willie's hands came out of his pocket, waving to shy away from the invitation. "Oh, no, thanks. I don't have to. I came to tell you..." His feet shuffled, but his eyes didn't leave Vicky. "I wanted to make sure you know I read your article."

Vicky returned forward from her backward step. Her stomach flipped completely over as Willie continued.

"That is, I've been reading all of yours, when they come out. They're good. But this last one..." He faltered over a voice that was going somewhat hoarse, requiring him to clear his throat. "I read it with my dad. I mean—we sat down and, um, yeah. We read it." He held up two of his fingers. "Twice. Then we talked more about my mom. For a few hours, I think."

Vicky's eyes grew during that personal disclosure. "Oh..." she breathed, bringing a hand to her chest, where the fluttering seemed to be migrating. Its essence changing.

Willie hesitated, and then he was the one to take a forward step, standing right before the doorway's threshold, his voice lowering. "It's something how you did that. The way you wrote it. You know?" Though the smile he had now didn't wobble, his voice did, a glisten slipping into his eyes. "Man! Honey Girl. If you keep...*doing* stuff like this, I—" After he cut himself off with a single, faint burst of a watery laugh, he reached up to scratch at the side of his head. "If you keep it up, I'm never gonna get the score even."

It was possible that, in response to his shortened moniker for her, a rosy tinge might have risen beneath the honey brown of Vicky's cheeks. Yet, a more definite response took place in her heart, on account of how Willie was expressing his. In this way of his.

Now, Vicky wasn't known for gushing forth with major reactions toward people. She had no reputation that would caution others to be on their guard while speaking to her. Moreover, she was no featherweight of a girl.

But Willie still had the trained reflexes of an athlete on his side, if that might have helped. Either way, he indubitably had Vicky beat in the area of physical strength and size.

Nature allowed that when such a heart-stirred Vicky would take a leap at such a large Willie with sudden momentum, the Willie wouldn't topple over.

And he didn't. His feet maintained a sufficiently steady plant on the ground as Vicky jumped up and embraced him around the neck with her arms, holding on tight. She wasn't sure if it was a laugh or a sob or a blend of both that bounced out of her then. "Willie."

Likely for both of them, his big bump right smack into her in the middle of Bro Brown's and the prolonged seconds that had come after that, followed some time later by his and her evening of dancing together, had afforded them some preparation for this. As for Vicky, nothing felt the least bit foreign or anything about Willie's hands clasping her around her back. Holding her close, holding her up, while she was in the midst of finding out a little more.

More about what Willie could feel. More about what she could too, and how it could be when feelings like this, from two different people, came together to become something mutual.

Granted, if Vicky had paused to think about it, she wouldn't have had English at the moment to describe what she was finding out, but that didn't matter. Not even in light of the writer she was growing to become.

At any rate, it so happened that Willie was holding her up in quite a literal sense. Vicky's feet hadn't come back to the ground after her jump.

Something of a rasp but more of a laugh was in Willie's voice as he said, "But anyway, maybe we can finally go get that vanilla malt I owe you, at least. Huh?" He leaned to set her down on her feet but didn't end their hug. "Or chocolate?"

Vicky drew back just enough to see his face clearly, and mischief coated the further suggestion he offered. "Or a pink cow?"

As her head briefly dipped, Vicky's following observation floated through a smile on her lips. "You were listening."

Willie released her at last, chuckling as he ran a knuckle—a drying knuckle?—underneath each of his glimmering eyes. "Eavesdropping, that time," he confessed.

Vicky laughed as well, holding up a finger asking him to wait, and she dashed away from the door. She made haste in gathering up her books from the couch and the living room floor, packing them back into her canvas bag for the time being and hurrying upstairs to her room with them. As much as she could hurry while hauling books.

A minute later, she was bounding downstairs with her hair freshly smoothed to keep from looking a mess, and she announced into the house's air, "Mom! I'm going out with Willie!"

Once she was back at the front door, getting into her coat with Willie's assistance, it wasn't her mother's voice that called back from somewhere upstairs. "All right—but no runnin' around!"

An alert, quizzical quirk came to Willie's eyebrows. "Uh...what'd he say?"

Vicky swept a hand backward across the air. "Ooh, nothing," she assured Willie with a singsong chortle before the two of them left the house.

Not long into their walk down the street, Willie sought out Vicky's hand with his, and she was more than happy to have her hand found. It wasn't until they reached their destination, where a few of the people who were already there turned to glance or stare, that it occurred to Vicky how this momentous occasion must look from the outside.

She was walking into Bro Brown's Burgers and Malts at the height of lunch hour, holding hands with West Hill's high school football star, who was correspondingly clad in his letterman jacket.

Yet, she wasn't with this guy because he was a star athlete. Not even because he was Willie with the Beard. Vicky was with him simply because he was Willie. So, when their entrance drew its share of attention, she took it in stride.

Their coming here to get the treat Willie "owed" her turned out to be a full lunch ordered for each of them. Their order included a request to "hold the onions," for whatever reason.

Vicky went on to spend that mealtime sitting in a booth across a table from Willie, jump blues music jumping from the jukebox while she found out still more for the afternoon. On one of the subjects they conversed over, Willie made a convincing case, proving to Vicky that vanilla wasn't the only suitable flavor of beverage to dip potato fries in. The chocolate malt on his side of the table and the top of the strawberry ice cream soda on her side were each worthy of potato fry dipping, she learned.

At some point during Willie and Vicky's time of burgers and banter, she was halfway sure that she caught a glimpse of Brother Brown flashing a grin their way, doing so through one of the windows in the kitchen doors behind the front counter.

Only halfway sure of that, she was.

Vicky and Willie didn't rush at all through their lunch. They also took their time on the walk back to her house. Once the two of them reached her front stoop, she considered that the longer they stood there, the greater the chance that one neighborhood passerby or another might do some gawking. Oddly enough, that thought wasn't enough to press Vicky into any hurry to go inside, so she had no qualms when Willie turned to face her and took her free hand, now holding both of hers in his.

As he moved in closer, bringing his temple to a light rest against hers, he began to sway. It was only natural for her to begin swaying right along with him to the rhythm of low humming in his throat.

Low humming that alluded to sentimental reasons.

Mmm. Music. A language with which to synchronize the rhythm of one's soul.

Or two souls.

Vicky swayed on with her favorite dance partner. Eventually, though, in regard to a matter her soul cared nothing about, her ears became fully aware.

Willie's humming voice was nowhere near the category of velvet or liquid chocolate. In fact, with every changing note, he was only a notch away from sliding off key entirely.

To keep from laughing, Vicky had to draw back a little. She looked up at Willie, who might have seemed for a second like he was on the verge of laughing too.

Then, all at once, no such verge was anywhere to be found. Willie stopped humming. Stopped swaying. Stood there holding Vicky's hands as he stared back at her.

Now, even at this stage of her personal life experience, she had her modest share of knowledge about what teenaged boys often bestowed upon teenaged girls. Again, Vicky had heard of boys bringing corsages to their dates for dances. She'd also been told that at a serious point in their relationships, some boys gave girls their ID bracelets.

What was more, she'd heard that at the end of a date, there was some likelihood that a boy would give a girl a goodnight kiss.

Well, perhaps there was a minor dilemma here, on that score. Vicky was positive that what she'd just gone on with Willie was indeed a date. However, given that this hour of the day didn't qualify as nighttime, a goodnight kiss was out of the question.

Hmm...

Then again, at the end of an afternoon date, a "see you later" kiss might be the perfect thing. She could urge Willie ahead in that vein, couldn't she?

With soft hints of a smile, Vicky gave her face a further tip upward, giving Willie's hands a squeeze to encourage him. Accordingly, hope filtered into what became his...somewhat drowsy look? Somewhat moonstruck?

The slow, careful lowering of his head afforded Vicky time. Time to let her eyes slip to a close before Willie's lips gently touched down on hers.

Oh! My. She leaned into the touch, having no wish to somehow get that returning inner fluttering of hers to go away. She was too busy finding something out.

The warm, lingering kiss Vicky shared with Willie was more than anything she'd quite been able to imagine. Definitely not a moment that had ever come to her mind in her younger days, back when she and a certain boy from the neighborhood used to go noisily running around outside, doing a bunch of nothing.

Here, now, was the pure joy of discovering how an innocent, noisy nothing could someday turn into such a new, wonderful something.

Something well worth finding out about. And that was the truth.

Author's Note

MUCH OF THE TIME, I can be rather old-fashioned.

I love watching vintage movies and television programs, and I also enjoy my share of vintage novels. That includes young adult "malt shop" books, which were published from the 1940s to the mid-1960s.

Malt shop books typically have storylines that are fairly light (sometimes medium) in weight. They feature young heroines navigating teenage life, without content like profanity, sex, or graphic violence. The stories often have a romantic focus or at least a side of romance in the overall mix.

So far in my reading, my old-fashioned self has generally found malt shop fiction to be pleasurable. Even so, there are fairly common moments when simply trying to relax in my nostalgic heart-and-head space isn't so easy for me as a Black American woman.

Unsurprisingly, among other problematic issues that can arise from indulging in entertainment from times past, one issue regarding malt shop fiction is its lack of racial diversity.

From what I've seen in the world of malt shop books, girls and guys of color are largely nonexistent. That is, they either don't exist in a substantial way, or they don't exist at all, for the most part.

Granted, I've come across a few young adult novels from that publishing period that do include or mention one or two persons of color, or that make direct or indirect references to race. Yet, during my reading, the majority of those inclusions or references didn't strike me as the most culturally competent or sensitive. (Or authentic, in one instance.)

I'd have to ask myself, "Do I wish this was another book that just didn't mention people of color at all, rather than mentioning them...like this?"

A Matter of Representation

—

TO STATE THE OBVIOUS, people of color did indeed exist in real-life America during the 1940s to mid-1960s (and during every other period, of course). Whole human beings with whole lives. Including teenagers.

Now, you may or may not be thinking what I often hear some people say—statements along the lines of: "You can't approach olden-day entertainment with modern-day social sensitivities or wishes. It was just a different time, back then."

However, I don't point out issues like this in relation to vintage fiction because I wish to somehow change the past. I point out the issues because, as the adage goes, those who cannot remember the past are condemned to repeat it. We should be aware of the past and be mindful not to wind up reverting or slipping back into former trends of racial exclusion and/or deficient racial representation in fiction genres that should be welcoming for a diverse range of peoples.

Also, just because circumstances were a certain way in "a different time, back then" doesn't mean everyone back at that time was perfectly happy or fine with it.

Narrowing this down to my Black culture for now, many Black Americans have *always* wanted more or better than what the wider society granted or permitted them. Many Black Americans have always cared about issues pertaining to their human dignity and social representation.

But they haven't always had the opportunities or platforms for their voices to be heard about it. At times when some did get their voices out there, much of America wasn't ready to listen or willing to budge that far from the status quo.

This isn't a new issue for Black Americans. Our desire to be represented well—especially to have the opportunities to represent *ourselves* well—isn't a desire that just recently popped up due to modern-day social sensitivities.

A Novel Idea

—

ONE RECENT TIME WHILE I was in my nostalgic space, getting into a malt shop novel, I ran into some non-malicious but racist humor in the story. That day, I just wasn't in the mood to do as I've often done with vintage entertainment: spit out a cherry pit and press on through the dessert, when I'd hoped at first to have one of those nice times when I could simply enjoy a good ol' dish of cherries jubilee. Sweet and pit-free.

I set the book aside. I still wanted to read something from the malt shop world, but you never know when one of those vintage books might have some of those pits in them.

Not long after that, on a couple of my jaunts around the internet, I came across some old photographs that were taken inside of soda and malt shops and ice cream parlors in the '40s through the '60s. One of the photos showed high school or college students: a few of them waiting at the front counter near the soda fountain, one of the girls standing and sipping a soft drink, and other students surrounding the shop's jukebox.

And what did those particular, old photographs I found all have in common? The people pictured in them were Black.

Some of them working, serving the customers.

Some of the customers sitting and chatting over their orders.

Some of them smiling or apparently laughing.

Certain ones stopping to stand together and smile right at the cameras.

Various groups of Black people. Malt-shopping like everyday Americans. Because they *were* everyday Americans.

An idea was coming to me. Fast.

Not at all for the first time in my bookish life, there was a certain kind of book I wanted to read but couldn't find, so I was going to have to write that book myself.

In this case, it would be a light-to-medium-weight story set during the malt shop era, centered on a cast of young Black American characters.

IN *Vicky's Victory*, the community of West Hill, nicknamed the Black Diamond district, is fictional, located in the equally fictional city of Port Milestone. While imagining West Hill, I was inspired by at least five different Black American communities in history.

To name two of them: 1) the Black Elite, also called the Black Aristocracy, of New York City during the Gilded Age, and 2) the self-sufficient, prosperous Greenwood neighborhood in Tulsa, Oklahoma during the early 20th century.

At that latter time, Greenwood was home to many middle- and upper-class Black Americans. The community was nicknamed Black Wall Street, with its own Black professionals and business owners; its own schools, including a business college; and its own newspaper.

(And yes, Black Wall Street was also where the Tulsa Race Massacre of 1921 occurred. An atrocity you should look up, if you haven't heard of it before.)

The historical fiction I usually write is non-magical historical fantasy, set in a completely fictional world. So, with this malt shop tale set in a fictional locale but in the real USA, I'd be writing my first work of straight-up historical fiction.

Proper and Proud

—

WHILE VICKY AND THE people of her community might or might not have technically capitalized the term "Black" in reference to their culture, I've capitalized the term for today's readers. When "Black" is capitalized, it's a proper noun that indeed refers to a *culture*, rather than a common noun that refers to color.

Moreover, in Chapter Three, Willie makes a reference to "race music." At the time, it was a term the music industry used to categorize Black American music, including blues, jazz, and gospel music. While much of segregated America refused or stayed away from race music for racist reasons, Willie doesn't use the term in a racially negative sense.

For many Black Americans in his day and earlier, "race" was a term of dignity, as Black Americans would proudly refer to themselves as "the Race."

Not many years after the point in time of this book, the music industry replaced the "race music" name with "rhythm and blues."

Malt Shop Milestones

—

NOW, AT THE TIME OF this writing, I've stepped out of my authorial norm by calling *Vicky's Victory* the first book in a series. Normally, I don't publicly designate or announce a "series" until I've at least started writing a second book already.

In this case, the book cover design and my purpose for writing Vicky's story very much called for the inclusion of a series name. So, I decided not to put off declaring the Malt Shop Milestones series.

I'm looking forward to spending more time in West Hill to continue writing about its people, including some newcomers. I already love it here!

Soundtrack!

—

Be sure to check out the Malt Shop Milestones series page for
the link to the classic jazz and blues songs in
Vicky's Victory.

Go to "Nadine's Books" at
www.prismaticprospects.wordpress.com

Young lives. First loves. And a classic American period enlivened by jukeboxes and chocolate malts.
Don't miss the next book in the
Malt Shop Milestones series!

Berta's Bounceback

To find all of Nadine's books and her blog featuring book reviews as well as posts on writing, diversity, films, and more, visit:

www.prismaticprospects.wordpress.com